WHY DIAMOND HAD TO DIE

RICHARD BURNS

WHY DIAMOND HAD TO DIE

BLOOMSBURY

F
Burns

First published 1989
Copyright © 1989 by Richard Burns

Bloomsbury Publishing Ltd, 2 Soho Square, London W1V 5DE

British Library Cataloguing in Publication Data
Burns, Richard, *1958–*
Why Diamond had to die.
I. Title
823'.914[F]
C291
ISBN 0-7475-0275-7

Photoset by Rowland Phototypesetting Ltd
Bury St Edmunds, Suffolk
Printed and bound in Great Britain by
Butler and Tanner Ltd, Frome and London

Jack Diamond lost interest in the Republican cause the day he was taking a leak in O'Malley's outside privy and the whole house blew up. If O'Malley had applied for the right improvement grants that would have been it for our lad. Now, in spite of his slightly dodgy past in the INLA, Jack's rubbing along quite nicely in London with the help of the DHSS and some lucrative victories at the snooker table. Then Flaherty turns up. Seems there's a little delivery job needs doing – a few days in Rome, nothing fancy, and that way Jack's Da will stay alive. What's he got to lose? Nothing – until Mulligan shows up too, sporting gun and balaclava, and things start to get complicated.

By the time we discover why Diamond *did* have to die, he'll have got drunk in Greece, got hijacked in North Africa, got shot in Paris, got laid in Rome, and got home just slightly ahead of the game. But not for long . . .

This is a splendidly entertaining thriller – fast-paced, exciting, funny, and a little sad.

**TO MICHELLE AND CHRISTIAN,
WHO CAN READ THIS WHEN THEY ARE OLDER**

ONE

Just another November morning, with the wind blowing round the shaft, shoving at the leaves, and the leaves too wet to move. I'm with the leaves there. I'm too wet to move. Too wet, too lazy, and too hampered by the furlong or so of rope Connor's lads have wrapped me in.

What I could do with is a cigarette. I'm meant to have given up smoking, but there's a laugh: what's the point of looking after my health when I'm about to be permanently entombed in one of the concrete piles supporting an M25 slip road? There are those, I suppose, who'd consider it an honour to become an integral part of Britain's motorway network, but I'm not among them. It isn't as if I'll be here that long, not like one of those bodies dug from peat bogs – Grauballe Man or Tollund Man – that look like tree roots with human faces and have been preserved for three thousand years. I'll just be Leatherhead Man, trussed up like a roll of old underlay and rediscovered in about eight months' time when the juggernauts have juddered the flyover to bits and the Department of the Environment condemns it.

I can hear voices and the sounds of machinery. The voices are friendly and human, and I'd call out if it wasn't that Connor and the boys had thoughtfully put a pair of socks in my mouth and secured them with a roll of Sellotape round my head. I fancy struggling – anyone would – but can't manage more than a wriggle; wriggling is just plain undignified so I decide to lie still. Lying I can cope with. Lying I am good at. It was lying got me into this mess in the first place.

It began that day in April when Flaherty came to see me. I was living in London at the time and it was a surprise to see Flaherty there. Flaherty was an acquaintance of my dad's: he was big in the Republican movement; he was big anywhere.

'Jack,' he said, when we'd exchanged the hellos and how-are-yous. 'How's your commitment to the cause?'

'So-so,' I replied, which wasn't exactly true. I'd given up on the cause, for good, the day O'Malley had blown himself, his wife and his three kids to smithereens, which was the same day I'd got this scar on my neck and nearly been atomized to boot. There are those who'll tell you outside privies are squalid, sordid and detrimental to your health. Don't listen to them. If O'Malley had been a bit smarter, if O'Malley had applied for the right improvement grants, I'd have been having a pee in a warm hygienic inside loo when the house went up. Instead I was in an open shed in the back yard, hosing down the cracked enamel, and I survived.

Either Flaherty was a bit of a mind-reader or it was obvious what I was thinking. 'Indeed, O'Malley was a fine fellow.'

'He was,' I said.

'One of the best,' said Flaherty.

'One of the best,' I agreed. This was getting plain daft though, because O'Malley had been about as much use as a walkman to the ghost of Anne Boleyn and we both knew it. But Flaherty wouldn't drop the subject.

'Gave his life for his country,' he said.

'He nearly took me with him,' I pointed out.

'A martyr to the cause,' expanded Flaherty, 'and you nearly a martyr with him.'

I remembered O'Malley's funeral. I was carrying his coffin. Have you ever worn a balaclava with two holes cut for the eyes? Have you ever tried attending a wake dressed like that? It was like some Irish joke: there we were, the six of us, wondering how to drink whiskey through the wool and whether we'd maybe look like idiots if we pulled the eyeholes down to our mouths. As if I wasn't having enough trouble anyway, with my neck all bandaged. Some of the old ones wanted to touch my wound: 'tis a fine and honourable thing this shedding of blood for the cause, they told me, though what was honourable about being rained with roof slates while having a pee I don't know.

But I was dwelling on the past, a bad habit of the Irish, and so I pulled myself up short and asked Flaherty what it was he wanted.

'We've a little job we think you should be doing.'

'What kind of job?' I hoped he would hear the reluctance in my voice.

'Just a small delivery. On the Continent. You'll be getting a free holiday out of it.'

'Delivering what?'

'Just something small. Small, innocuous, and very, very important. I want you to know that. Very, very important.'

'Then why pick me?' I asked. 'I haven't been active for years.'

'To be sure and that's the reason you're our choice,' said Flaherty. He had always affected these stage Irishisms, though he was a Derryman like me. 'You're clean. It's nine years since O'Malley died. You've done well for yourself, got yourself an education, lost yourself an accent almost. You don't sound Irish; you don't even have an Irish-sounding name.'

Well, all of that was true. There hadn't been much time for school when I was a lad, what with lobbing half-bricks at the Specials and dodging the plastic bullets, but since O'Malley's death I'd started to read a lot, poetry mostly, and somehow it had gone on from there: night school, exams, place as a mature student at an English university, degree. And he was right about my name. Diamond doesn't sound Irish, though Diarmid, which is what it was before my grandfather went to England and got confused, certainly does. Dear Granda, despite being able to find his mouth three times out of five when he raised his glass, wasn't so good at the spelling: he entered England with one name, came out with another and decided he preferred the new one. God bless him, he even called his daughters Sapphire and Emerald in case anyone missed the point, which is probably why they married so young.

So I nodded sagely at Flaherty to show I understood his reasoning, and prayed that if he needed me clean he would keep me clean.

'What am I delivering?' I asked.

'It's a liaison job. We want a little parcel taking to a man in Rome.'

'What's in the parcel?'

'Nothing. A book.'

'All right. And what's in the book?'

Flaherty laughed. 'My! Aren't we suspicious!'

'Too bloody right I am,' I said. 'I've no desire to end my days in an Italian prison.'

'The book is as innocent as a new-born babe,' he said. Where I was born even the babies wear green and chuck pebbles at the RUC, but I let this pass. 'You'll be doing it for us?'

'Have I any choice?'

He laughed again, the grey skin wobbling round his eyes. 'Don't be like that. It's for the cause. Though I should warn you that we know where your father is.'

This was hardly a surprise. My da lived on the same street he always had, one along from Flaherty himself. I raised my eyebrows a notch.

'Exactly,' nodded Flaherty. 'So it wouldn't be hard to send a couple of the lads to see him now, would it?'

'So that's the way it is, is it?'

'Now don't get me wrong, son. I just want to emphasize how important this little job is to us. Not difficult,' he said, heading off my next, half-formed objection. 'Just important. Message received?'

'I suppose so.'

'Good. Because if you don't get it, your da will.'

'Do you want any other assurances?' I asked. 'My left hand preserved in brine for when I get back, maybe? A string round my balls to stop me straying?'

'You've always had spirit,' said Flaherty. 'Ever since you was a lad. One more thing. We'll want to borrow your car while you're away.'

'How do you know I've got a car?' I asked, which was a daft question.

'Red Vauxhall, registration number XLK94X, tax running out next week. Get that fixed by the way; we wouldn't want any trouble with the constabulary now.'

'Sure, my pleasure. What do you want it for?'

This was an even stupider thing to ask. Flaherty gave me a pitying look. 'Report it stolen when you get back,' he said, and moved on to the next point. 'We've booked a fortnight for you in Greece. Package job: flight, half-board, nice hotel next to the beach. It really is a shame you'll not be staying there, but we've got a ringer in for you. You, Jack, will be flying on directly from Thessalonika to Rome without leaving the airport, collecting your ticket from a friend of ours over there. You'll also be given an address. You're going between two EEC countries so you can travel on your own passport: you'd never believe what we have to pay for forgeries these days.'

It sounded unnecessarily complicated but what the hell, who was I to tell them how to conspire? Suddenly Flaherty reached in his pocket like a man going for a gun and pulled out a package-holiday wallet, full of tickets and boarding passes and plastic tags to label your luggage. In the wallet was a handful of Greek picture postcards.

'You'll not be leaving for a fortnight,' he told me, 'but I'd like the postcards written now so we can get them off to our friend in Greece. He'll post them one a day. You know fourteen people to write to?'

'Come off it. I don't know fourteen people at all.'

'What about all the women? Sarah, isn't it? And Melissa and Louise and Kathy and Joanne. Pretty girls all of them: it's amazing they let you treat them the way you do. A touch of the blarney, eh?'

The vertical hold on my face needed adjusting: my eyebrows stayed up and my jaw dropped down. 'You know how it is,' I said, going for an airy tone and producing a strangled one.

'And you a good Catholic boy as well. What would Father Thomas say?'

As Father Thomas had pawed every girl in the Bible class, and half the mothers as well, I expect he'd have wished me luck. 'What do I do for money?' I asked. 'I'm not rich.' Which was like saying the Pope's not Jewish.

'You'll get expenses.'

'Decent expenses?'

'Expenses. Now, if you could just be writing a postcard or two I'll be saying goodbye.'

I fetched my address book and sat on the bed, resting the cards on the ironing board. The board had a spongy cover, decorated with purple hyacinths; the cover gave under my pen and made writing laborious.

Flaherty stood over me as I wrote. 'What about this one?' he suggested, pointing at a number scrawled in lipstick over a two-page spread.

'I've never even phoned her, if it's the one I think it is. She's from Macclesfield and I couldn't be bothered to look up the code.'

'This one then?'

'It's a possibility; I suppose I could drop her a line.' Actually, it seemed rather a good idea. She was a lovely girl and I hadn't seen her in months. What's she doing tonight, I wondered: I might well give her a ring. But it was at this moment that the man with the gun in his hand came through the door. He was a big man. He didn't need a coat hanger for his jacket, he needed an aircraft hangar, and he was wearing one of those bloody stupid balaclava affairs. I wondered if he'd walked down the street dressed like that. What were the neighbours going to say? More pressingly, what was he going to say? He didn't keep us waiting for long.

'Flaferfy,' he said, talking like that because of the balaclava. 'Flaferfy, we've been looking for you.'

'Mulligan?' asked Flaherty, his face white. 'Is it you?'

'And who else would it be being?' He took off his balaclava. He was a man in his late thirties, dark, and very ugly. His face looked as though it had been used as a football by a platoon of military policemen, which was a coincidence because it had.

'How did you know I was here?'

'I've been following you for a while, Flaherty. You shouldn't have stopped off at the pub on the corner. Word was sent.'

Ah, I thought: the pub on the corner. The Hare and Pheasant – the Tar and Feather as it's known round here – full of miserable Irishmen celebrating their nation's defeats over the Guinness. Ah, the dear old Tar and Feather. Its very name seemed an oasis of sanity amidst the troubles which had walked unannounced into my life. I started to say something along these lines, just to raise the tone of the conversation, but got about as far as the first 'Ah' before Mulligan shut me up with a wave of his gun.

'You can guess what I want,' said Mulligan to Flaherty.

'I can't,' replied Flaherty. He was recovering himself now, maybe because the gun was pointing at me.

'Come on! We know all about the Cairo Accord.'

'I don't understand,' said Flaherty, but he was bluffing and we all knew it. He looked about as hopeful as a man trying to sell a Skoda.

'Don't play games with me. We know about the Accord and we want in.'

'Who's "we"?' asked Flaherty, playing for time, because he knew as well as I did. Officially Mulligan and Flaherty were meant to be part of the same organization, the Irish National Liberation Army, but that meant nothing. There were as many cracks in the INLA as in the Bumper Book of Jokes, and it was about as funny. In the good old days in the seventies, when I'd worn a black balaclava and Seamus Costello had been in charge, the INLA had been a fighting unit. But in 1977 Costello had been gunned down by the IRA, and though the INLA was still fighting, no way was it a unit. Flaherty was from the Derry Brigade, Mulligan from Belfast.

'You know who!' replied Mulligan, interrupting my thoughts again. 'Where's the fucking book?' They don't mince words, these terrorists.

Now Flaherty really was astonished: he looked like a man who had *sold* a Skoda. 'You know about that?'

'Of course we do. We know a lot about you, Flaherty. You and your friend, the British lord. Now where's the book?'

'Hidden,' said Flaherty.

'I know it's hidden. Where?'

'I don't know.'

'I'll blow your fucking head off.' Mulligan's voice was as hard as a prick at a peepshow.

'I don't know but I can find out.'

'You'll do better than that. You'll tell me.'

'I am telling you! I don't know where it is! I'll find out!'

'How?'

'Just one telephone call! That's all it'll take! Honest!'

'Make it.'

Nobody asked if Flaherty could use my phone because nobody needed to. I was still looking down the muzzle of Mulligan's gun. The mouth of hell was .45 of an inch in diameter and gaped like the Mersey tunnel. Flaherty dialled.

'Hello? Mr Smith? Mr Green from the Export Division here. Now, before I get any further I want you to take note of this: there's a man in Los Angeles we might have a bit of a problem with . . . Yes, that's right. In Los Angeles. In LA . . . Oh, for Pete's sake, write it down. I want you to ring him up right away. I want you to give him a bell, fast. Got it . . . ? Now, I've forgotten where the book is kept and would really like to find out . . . It's where . . . ? Oh, I see. Right, thanks.'

Clever bloke, Flaherty, thinking on his feet. I don't have to spell out the 'In LA/INLA' bit, much less 'Bell fast'; it's obvious to all but a moron. Fortunately Mulligan was a moron. 'It's in a safe deposit box on High Holborn,' said Flaherty. 'We can't get it till the morning. Well, I'll be off to bed.'

'Stay where you are!' Mulligan's gun rose to Flaherty's face. 'We'll be waiting together.'

'Have it your own way,' said Flaherty with a shrug. He turned to me. 'Have you got a spare room?'

I had a bedsit, as was obvious from the fact that we were sitting

8

on the bed, facing the kitchen sink and writing postcards on the ironing board. 'I'm afraid not,' I told him.

'Pity. Well, I'll just rest here. Why don't you lie on the floor?'

'Lie on the floor?' I asked.

'*Lie on the floor!*'

Oh. He wants me to lie on the floor! 'Sure,' I said. 'Fine.' And I did as I was asked. Flaherty reclined on the bed. He'd got his composure back entirely; he'd received the money for the Skoda in cash. We settled down for the wait.

Time passed slowly. I was dozing, composing limericks in my head to while away the hours: There was a young gunman called Mulligan . . . There was an old bastard called Flaherty. Considering the Irish invented limericks, we surely didn't make the rhymes easy. Mulligan/Hull again. Flaherty/latter tea/Saturday, if you stretched it. What day is it anyway, I wondered, virtually asleep by now. Tuesday? That's right, Tuesday. It must be: I signed on this morning. Giro in the post on Thursday, three blissful days of wine and eleven days left to sleep it off before the next payday. Unless I get to Rome . . . I was just wondering whether *dolce* was Italian for the dole when the gunfire started.

Two of them came in through the window, a third through the door. Their silenced pistols spat ugly noises above my head. I watched Mulligan's face split open and saw him crumple on to the ironing board.

My ironing board was designed by the same psychopath who invented deckchairs, and under Mulligan's weight it fell over, collapsed and folded. Flaherty yelled as it caught his hand.

I'd heard that the Brits had kicked the shit out of Mulligan, but this wasn't true if the stench now was anything to go by. He lay next to me on the floor, half on and half off the ironing board, with his cheek a mess of split bone and his jaw dangling on threads of flesh; Flaherty lay on the bed with his hand mangled up in the board and screamed and screamed.

Two

It was a lousy wet night in the thirty-eighth year of the reign of Elizabeth II. The gunmen showed me politely but firmly out of my bedsit: 'Fuck off, cunt,' they told me. I can take a hint.

It was dark out. Headlamps interrogated the streets. I walked slowly, damply, and the rain fell steadily. It was like an Irish terrorist, this rain: invisible in the shadows, thick in front of the lights. I'd bought my watch from a service station: it was one of those fancy quartz things that can wake you with a choice of three different squeaky tunes or split a second a hundred ways, but the battery was dodgy and it couldn't be relied on for the time. The closed doors of the Tar and Feather told me it was late, too late. That was a pity; I'd been given two hours to kill while the professionals disposed of the body, or whatever it was they had to do.

I made my way east through littered London, stepping over the drunks, avoiding the hard-eyed whores. A fast-food joint served me something that was neither fast nor food. A green cross announced an all-night chemist; so did the queuing junkies. Derelicts lit fires in derelict buildings. The taxis were rank with tobacco and grease. This is London calling, London calling . . . Hermann Goering couldn't have done a better job.

Stairs led me down to a basement. A neon sign announced 'Ginger's Snooker Emporium'. Don was on the door: he smiled his Atilla-the-Hun-on-a-good-day smile, and let me through. The hall was large and low. There was a bar at one end, where you could only buy crisps and soft drinks, since the magistrates had discovered Don selling booze all night long and Ginger's had lost its licence. I walked the length of the room. Drifting smoke turned all the colours pastel. I handed my coat in and hired a cue. 'Anyone in worth knowing?' I asked.

'Laddie on table four looks likely. Made a sixty break last frame.'

'Worth a look, you reckon?'

'Worth a game, I'd say.'

'Thanks.' I went over to table four. Frank Finlayson I recognized; the other, a youngster, was new to me. Frank's not a bad player, maybe a little cautious, but steady; the youngster was running rings round him. They were on to the colours. Frank was forty points adrift, with twenty-seven on the table, and as I watched the youngster potted a long yellow, screwed back to take a straight green, strutted round the table for the brown, put away the blue and lined up on the pink.

'Leave it, kid,' said Frank. 'Game's over.'

The youth nodded to show he'd understood and, cueing one-handed with the cue resting on the cushion, sank the pink anyway.

Frank turned to me. 'Watch this one,' he said. 'He's good.'

'How much have you made tonight?' I asked the youngster.

'Sixty quid.'

'Not bad. Care to risk that on a single game?'

The youngster thought hard. 'Best of three?' he suggested.

'I haven't time,' I told him, which wasn't true but I hadn't the patience for more. 'A single game or nothing.'

He shrugged. 'If you like.'

'I like.'

He tossed a coin. It glittered as it took off, disappeared into the shadows above the shaded lights and reappeared in his hands. 'Heads,' I said.

'Heads it is.'

'I'll break.' I lined up the white, an inch from the brown on the base-line, and struck it with firm right-hand side into the pack. It hit the second red down from the pink, ducked towards the pocket, came back up the table, and rolled to a stop behind the brown. A nice break.

The kid was almost up to it though, bouncing the cue ball off the side cushion and into the reds, giving it enough side to bring it back down the table. But a single ball was dislodged, a long shot into the top left-hand pocket. I took aim. My body was still; the only movement was in my swinging right forearm as I lined up my cue, the white, the red and the pocket in a single pure stroke; I made my shot. The red rattled in the jaws of the pocket and went in. The white nestled comfortably behind the black, with just enough angle to put me on to my next red.

Snooker is the perfect game. The green baize looks like grass and simulates some healthy outdoor sport. The coloured balls make patterns on the cloth, hieroglyphics to be read by those with a mind to know. But above all snooker is sex: wielding a firm cue, kissing and screwing, fitting the balls in the holes. Sex without AIDS: no wonder it's getting so popular. I potted the black, rolled the white into the pack and lined up my next red.

Now I was machine only, pumping out the shots, a calculator working out the angles. Red, black, red, pink. Screw back for a red, middle pocket, and back and back again for the respotted pink in the top left. But the break was over: I'd left no angle after a long red down the table and had to content myself with a nudge off the yellow which put him into baulk.

Thirty-one plays nil: a healthy lead but not enough, particularly when I was using a borrowed cue; I was betting money I hadn't got and the youngster was no mug.

He proved this with a lovely safety shot which rolled up the table, kissed a red tidily into the pack and returned to within an ace of where it had started from. I couldn't try the same shot: he'd moved the one spare red, so I rolled a gentle white into the pack. It was not gentle enough, and when he'd finished his break my thirty-one was overshadowed by his forty-six. Still, his last shot had been a poor one, an over-ambitious blue into the middle bag to bring him on to one of the remaining reds: he'd missed the blue but lined up on the red perfectly, and I dropped that one with ease. Thirty-two plays forty-six; fourteen in it but only three reds to re-establish my lead. I couldn't afford to take chances: I played a long safety shot off the pink and left the white at the other end of the table.

The hieroglyphics said CAUTION now, in letters three feet high. The black was on its spot, the pink halfway to the right cushion, and the reds comfortably distributed around them. Any mistake at this stage would cost a lot of points and I prayed he'd be the one to make it.

He played safe; I played safe. He was behind the brown now, middle of the table, with an impossible pot to go for, or a straightforward safety shot off the red on the bottom cushion. He went for the impossible red. Oh, the carelessness of youth, I thought, until he potted it.

After the red he took a black; after the black another red. The pink tempted a long shot to the top right-hand pocket but the last red was safe against the bottom cushion still. He smashed into the pink with a lot of side: the white came back into the red all right but the pink missed the pocket by a foot and came back down the table. I took the red and the black and the score was forty to me, fifty-five to him.

Yellow, green, blue and black were on their spots still: I went back down for the yellow, followed it with the green, but missed the maverick brown. He didn't. Fourteen in it, eighteen on the table. If he got the blue the game was over. He didn't and I did, screwing the white back for the pink, touching the pink and going very nicely in-off into the top left pocket. Five away: nineteen in it, eighteen on the table, the blue respotted and the white in hand. Where the fuck was I going to find sixty quid?

He lined up the blue. 'A bit of a pressure shot this, kid,' I told him helpfully, as he struck the white with a fluid action. 'Oh, hard luck.'

I needed a snooker now. The white was loose in the middle of the table, the black still on its spot, the pink at the other end of the table. I tapped the white gently into the blue. It hit the cushion and rolled gleefully behind the black. The blue snuggled up to the cushion. 'Good shot,' I told myself.

For the second time that frame his youth showed. Instead of playing off the angles he went for an ambitious swerve shot, but the cushion inhibited his action and the white squirted across the table. Five to me, and a free ball because the blue was still hidden. I played the pink, missed the shot, but left him snookered; he got out of it effortlessly this time, and the score was sixty-four to my fifty.

I got the blue and the pink. A black ball game, but the distance between the white and the black, after I had taken that pink, seemed daunting. I no longer felt like a snooker machine. The table was half a league long now, and the balls ridiculously small. I had a reasonably straight shot for the bottom right bag though, and had to go for it. I hit it too hard, caught the wrong angle, and missed the pocket by so much it was difficult to guess which one I was aiming for.

The black bounced off the side cushion hard. I thought it would maybe go into the opposite bottom pocket but instead it bounced off both angles and rolled towards the moving white in the middle of the table. I was setting him up here for a perfect straight shot into the middle left hole. The balls kissed gently. The white stopped on the blue spot; the black travelled slowly towards the pocket, touched the jaw, teetered over the hole, settled, rocked and dropped.

'Bloody hell,' said my opponent, with admirable restraint.

'Goodness me,' I said, feeling I must match him.

'Sixty quid,' said the youngster, offering me a handful of notes and change.

'Goodness me,' I repeated, still looking at the hole where the black had disappeared.

'Good game,' said the youngster. He was all right. I smiled at him.

'Make it thirty,' I said. 'I was bloody lucky.'

He smiled back. 'Thirty? What about a return game?'

'Haven't the time. Sorry. Next time I'm in, okay?'

'Sure.' He found three tenners in the bundle of money, pocketed them and gave me the rest. 'Next game I win, right?'

I didn't argue. I took my thirty quid, handed back the cue, picked up my jacket and left. I can't say I felt that wonderful: the snooker hall had been a useful way of making cash, and now that was over. I was getting old, that was clear. I should have taken all the money. The next time I went to Ginger's I'd have to play this lad again. Sixty quid that would cost me, sixty quid I still hadn't got. 'See you,' said Don as I left.

'Sure,' I said, but I lied.

The rain was heavier now, running off the guttering into the basement yard, tumbling down the steps like a drunk. I turned up my collar, grabbed at my lapels, and headed into the night. Still, I thought, thirty quid is thirty quid, and if I go to Maurie's I can manage a blinder on that. I might even find some susceptible young floozie with a room of her own if I'm lucky. So instead of turning left to go home, I turned right. Ethics has never been my strong point, but I can't be the first bloke to have found that right is wrong.

Not that things started badly. The air in Maurie's was no worse than usual, which means it was as rich, thick and sweaty as an Oxford rugby Blue; the dancers' hair was frayed by furtive light, the drinkers were getting high as the prices. I balanced on a bar stool and lit a cigarette. That way at least some of the smoke came through a filter.

'Hi, Jack,' said Gerry Duggan. Gerry ran the club. He was a short fat man who'd been cashiered from the Salvation Army. 'How're things?'

'Not so good, not so bad. And you?'

'Nicely-nicely. Haven't seen you for a while.'

'Blame monetarist economics. No money, screwed-up economy.'

Gerry poured me a drink. 'First one's on the house.'

'Cheers.'

Consider me unpatriotic if you will, but I've a fondness for Scotch. Irish whiskey is good, but there's something rougher about Scotch. Irish makes you feel good, Scotch lets you know you're a man. Not that I needed reminding. Maybe it was the proximity of all those women, but I had an erection as hard and awkward as Flaherty himself. It was as well the lights were dim. I turned and watched the dancers, looking for an eye to catch.

'Hello handsome.'

I half-knew this girl. Kelly, her name was, which was also the name of the man who kept the corner shop at the end of my da's street. 'Hello Kelly,' I said, and it damn near came out 'Hello Mr Kelly', like my old da had taught me to say.

'You buying a girl a drink?'

'Sure. Any girl in particular?'

'This one'll do fine.' She gave me the wide-eyed alluring look, both eyes on main beam.

'Just what I was thinking,' I assured her.

I wasted some time looking at my watch, and then checked with the clock behind the bar. I still had an hour to get rid of before I could go back home. So we had a drink, and then another, and maybe one or two more. We danced close, which is the only way you can dance in Maurie's, once the crowd gets in; and her blonde head, the roots barely showing, rested tight on my chest.

We found a bench seat behind a low table. I sat, Kelly knelt beside me. She put her arms round my shoulders and her tongue in my ear. 'Take me home with you,' she whispered, but there we had a bit of a problem.

Instead we went upstairs. Gerry kept a couple of quiet rooms that he let for a price or a friend. I used the key he had slipped me and let us in.

It was a practical sort of room. There was a mattress on the floor, with a clean sheet folded on it, and there was a rug by the mattress; the only light came from the red bulb hanging naked from the ceiling. It's tough being romantic when you have to make your own bed, but we did our best, wrestling our clothes off and the sheet on in a flurry of passion. We looked like a tumble-dryer turned inside out, and instead of getting drier we got wetter.

Our tongues darted and probed together, our busy hands caressed. She was hot and oiled and inviting, and that was only her mouth. I stroked her delicate secrets, urging her, exploring her, and her fingers gouged patterns in my back. 'Let lips do what fingers do,' said Romeo to Juliet, and Romeo knew a thing or two. Her breathing measured my success, coming in awkward gasps when I hit the button. 'Take me,' she said in a stage whisper, and I did, diving into her lubricated depths like a penguin after a fish.

Afterwards we had a wash and a ritual cigarette, and then she told me how old she was. 'Bloody hell!' I said.

'I've run away from home,' she explained. 'Can I live with you?'

'Let's give it a year or three, shall we? Till it's legal.'

'Not fair,' she said with a pout, and then smiled to show she didn't mean it. She certainly didn't act fourteen. I smiled back, put on my clothes and made to leave.

'Give the key back to Gerry when you've dressed,' I told her.

'Who says I'm getting dressed?' she asked, stretching her naked-ness on the rumpled sheet. 'I might just see who turns up here next. I haven't been in a threesome for weeks.' She ran her tongue along her upper teeth; I turned to go before there were any further offences to be taken into consideration.

'See you round,' I told her.

'Any time,' she replied. 'You're good.' She was an expert. But I had a deserted daughter her age in Derry. Who's screwing *her*, I wondered, then wished I hadn't.

The walk home from Maurie's took me along the canal. The water was black. A dead rat floated by, looking like a teabag with legs. A lighted barge was fragrant with marijuana. A condom hung from a bush. Discarded plastic bags, wrinkled and perished by the glue inside, wafted beneath the bridges. It was a still night. Yellow lamps reflected in the canal water. The eastern sky was lighter than the west. I left the canal and walked up an alley past the dustbins and old prams. No light penetrated the alley, and the darkness hurt. I thought of Kelly and my Marie, my daughter. I had lost by getting what I wanted; now all I wanted was out.

It was the girl who approached me first, a small white face

coming through the darkness. 'Got a light mate?' she asked, and though her London whine changed gear on the vowels I guess I was feeling sentimental; I guess I was thinking about my lost daughter.

'Sure.'

I reached in my pocket for my lighter, pulled it out and cupped a hand to shelter it from the rain. She bent her head over the light. I saw a pretty face with ugly skin, a sodden raincoat, a pair of knees, and then, from my new position on the ground while her boyfriend stood on my neck, got a really close look at her pointed black shoes.

'Frisk him,' instructed the boyfriend.

They found the single fiver I had left and didn't bother with the change. 'Come on!' said the girl, walking quickly down the alley.

'OK,' agreed the boyfriend, kicking me in the kidneys as he left. 'See you!' he called.

'I hope so,' I muttered, but he had gone, following her into the absolute dark.

I wondered what he had hit me with. Something heavy. Something really heavy, that was for sure. I counted ten. That didn't work. I tried twenty. Neither did that. Okay, okay, let's go for the ton. I lost it at forty-six or so, started again, and by the time I had actually made it to a hundred I'd forgotten what the counting was for. Oh well, what the hell. I was getting kind of comfy on the cobbles. I even resented it when the policeman picked me up.

'You'd better come with me,' he said. This sounded reasonable so I went along with it. 'Been drinking, have we, sir?' He was a polite policeman, the sort that asks questions first. I know. I've met the other sort as well.

'I've been mugged,' I told him.

'Well, we'll soon find out. Let's be having you. I'm taking you back to the station.'

The station was ridiculously close, just beyond the end of the alley. I was led in. The bright lights hurt my eyes, and the cream-painted walls, patched with posters of missing children and warnings to keep things locked, were reflecting the dangling light bulbs in urinous yellow pools.

'Drunk?' asked the sergeant.

'Might be,' replied the policeman, steering me to the desk. 'Reckons he's been mugged.'

'Don't they all? Name?' This was addressed to me.

'Jack Diamond. Sorry. John Michael Diamond.'

'Address?'

'44b Ottway Street, NW2.'

'All right. Sit him over there. He'll have to wait his turn.'

They put me in a canvas chair opposite the desk. I put my hand to my head: the hair was soaking and the scalp tender. I pulled my hand away, expecting blood, and saw none.

A policewoman collected my possessions. Three pound coins and a few coppers. My lighter. A packet of Benson and Hedges. My keys. 'Sign here.' I signed. 'Doctor'll be here in a minute. What's your story anyway?'

'I was mugged. Just down the alley behind this place. A girl and a bloke. Girl asked me for a light, bloke hit me.'

'They didn't take much money!'

'They took the notes.' I liked that plural: the policewoman wasn't bad-looking, come to look at her, and I felt like impressing. 'I'd just won thirty quid playing snooker.' No need to mention Maurie's.

'Playing snooker this time of night?'

She wasn't so good-looking either. I gave her up.

'You're in for drunk and disorderly,' she warned.

'Doctor'll soon clear that. I haven't had a drink all night.' Well, all right, so that wasn't quite true, but I hadn't had many, and a lot had happened since.

'If you say so.' She left: so much for the blarney. But there was a stained-glass window, all colours and pains, between my eyes and the world, so I reckoned I had an excuse.

The doctor came round. He was in a hurry. He smelt my breath. 'Seems clear.' He held up his fingers. 'How many?'

'Five.' I leaned forward, offering the back of my head to his professional judgement. 'I was mugged.'

The doctor fingered the lump. 'He's right!' he called. 'He's been hit on the head.'

'Could he have done it falling down?' asked the sergeant.

'Not much trace of alcohol on his breath. Do you have anything else on him? I'll give him a blood test if you like, but we've got the Bolton Wanderers fans to look at.'

'If you say it's not worth it we'll let him go. Does he need hospital?'

'Do you?' asked the doctor, leaving already.

'Do I?' I called after him, but he had gone. 'It seems not,' I told the sergeant.

'Right. You were mugged. We'll accept that. Make a statement and I'll get a car to drive you home.'

'I don't like to say I told you so,' I began, and then realized something. 'A car? Drive me home?'

'Yeah. What of it?'

Maybe there would have been a better way. Maybe if I'd thought about it I could have worked something a little less drastic. Instead I thumped him, full on the nose. There was no way I was going back to my bedsit in a police car: if Flaherty and his hitmen hadn't finished clearing up I'd be an accessory to murder; if they had they'd still be keeping an eye on the place and I'd rather be caught in a brothel by the Society of Jesus than seen with a policeman near there.

So I hit him, and four or five policemen hit me, and one of them trod on my hand, and I spent the night in a cell. I examined the damage as best I could, what with some stinking Scotsman mistaking me for a barmaid he'd known in Motherwell and some lousy Londoner singing 'Chicago' off-key. My face was kind of shapeless, my kidneys still ached where they'd been kicked, the first joint of each finger was bloated and blue. I thought about Flaherty's hand, trapped in my ironing board. Poor Flaherty: I hope it gives him hell.

THREE

The policeman was ridiculously young and his face was dotted with spots: he could have been spray-painted through a colander. 'You,' he said, which meant me. 'On your feet!' If I had a complexion like that I'd be aggressive too.

I climbed to my feet carefully, trying to remember what I'd been drinking. I'd not had a head like this in months. It was the lecherous Scot who reminded me. 'Gi'us a kiss, jimmy,' he said, and as I considered his request the world came into focus: crowded narrow bunks, bare bulbs, cream-painted brickwork, puffy raw bruises swelling the backs of my hands. I was in a cell. Unenthusiastic daylight peeked in through the barred window, didn't like what it saw, and looked away.

'Get yourself over here,' instructed the policeman. I tried to oblige but I was lame as a husband's excuse. By the time I reached him I was ready to fall over, which I did. He yanked me by the hair and pulled me up. 'You wanting sympathy, mate?' he asked. 'Go tell it to the Marines.'

'Marines?' I asked. He held my face six inches from his. I thought he was going to nut me, but instead he let me go. Perhaps he worried about what the impact would do to his acne.

I recovered a kind of balance. 'Where now?' I wondered.

'You'll see.'

He made it sound like a threat, so I was relieved only to be taken to the desk. I was even relieved to see Flaherty there, which was daft: I should have learned long ago that Flaherty was never anything except trouble. With him was a younger man whose well-cut business suit was disfigured by the bright badges he wore on his lapels: 'Red Wedge', 'Troops Out', 'Support the Knutsford Eight' and 'Free Nelson Mandela'. This didn't look like the English aristocrat mate of Flaherty's that Mulligan had mentioned; on the other hand, Flaherty in his brown suit and brown tie didn't look much like a terrorist.

'Diamond,' said Flaherty, his jowled grey face making no effort to smile. 'My name is Brian Fowles and this is Pete Joy. Pete is a solicitor.'

My name's Gunga-Din and I'm Vice-President of the USA. 'Pleased to meet you both,' I told them, shaking hands with Joy. I wanted to shake hands with Flaherty too, if only to tweak his well-bandaged fingers, but he didn't offer. Besides, my own hands, crustacean blues and pinks, couldn't have done justice to the job. 'How did you know where I was?'

Flaherty flashed his knowing look. 'We have our sources.'

'I gather there's been some harassment,' said Joy complacently. He was young, though not as young as he wanted to be, and wore a Zapata moustache. 'We're here to see that there's been no infringement of your rights.'

'Mr Joy is on the local police committee,' said Flaherty, like a man whose dog can do tricks.

'He fell down the steps to the cell,' put in the spotty policeman, which was rich, for there were no steps to the cell.

'Is that so?' mused Flaherty. 'Well, as I don't suppose you'll be charging this young man we'll not need to investigate that, will we?'

He was all charm; I was particularly impressed by that 'young man' line, though I suspect it said more about Flaherty's age than mine.

'Well, we haven't charged him yet,' acknowledged the policeman.

'Good. Then there'll be no trouble. Can he have his possessions?'

I checked them and returned them to my pockets. 'That everything?' asked Joy.

'Yes.'

'You're absolutely certain?'

'Yes.'

'Positive? Nothing missing?'

What did he want me to say? I didn't know so I couldn't say. The young policeman showed us the door. 'Good morning,' he said as we left. 'Nice doing business with you.'

We drove off in Joy's Mazda, Flaherty's width squashed in the front, and me in the back like a kid on an outing. 'How did you swing that so easily?' I asked their shoulders.

Joy replied. 'Carrot and stick. I'm a radical lawyer; I'm the stick. The carrot was a bit of cash. No bother. But why did you lay one on the policeman at the desk in the first place?'

'Shall I tell him?' I asked Flaherty.

'Leave out the details.'

'I'd been mugged. The police offered me a lift back to my room. I thought Mr Flaherty . . .'

'Mr Fowles,' corrected Flaherty.

'Mr Fowles here might not want the police around. I couldn't think of anything else to do so I hit the copper.'

'Rather extreme,' said Joy. 'That could have been awkward. It's a good thing they beat you up.'

'Absolutely wonderful,' I told him. 'Just marvellous.' No matter which way I sat, it hurt. We were driving south and east, past Hyde Park and into Piccadilly. 'Where are we going?' I asked. 'I thought you were taking me home.'

'Actually, we don't think home's a very good idea for a little while,' said Flaherty. 'You've put us in a difficult position. Why did you go to the police in the first place?'

I explained. They were unimpressed. We drove through White-hall and crossed the river.

'You should have telephoned a lawyer immediately,' said Joy, changing gear above the oily waters of the Thames.

'I don't know any lawyers.'

He handed me his card without taking his eyes from the road.

Toole, Joy Associates, Radical Law. 'In future, get in touch with me.'

'It won't happen in future,' I said. Flaherty spoke simultaneously. I wasn't quite sure what he said, but it sounded uncomfortably like 'He hasn't got a future.'

Our route was roundabout. We drove past Waterloo station, following the river, and then back across London Bridge, which was snarled up with the early morning traffic. We continued north, threading our way through the City: if we were sightseeing we were missing the sights. We passed King's Cross and touched the edge of Regent's Park. Snowdon's aviary was an old hairnet hung from a pole; the canal boats wore their gaudy cheerful colours like the madames of brothels. Looking down towards the park, I saw a camel crossing the road: who says the Arab influence in London is on the wane? Finally we reached a back street north of Camden.

'Safe house,' said Joy, letting me out. He seemed to relish the conspiratorial phrase.

'Thanks for your help,' said Flaherty from the pavement. We were on the edge of the market. The air was stale with cabbages and diesel. Two blacks on roller skates went by, hand in hand. Another walked the other way, with one of those portable stereos that can exactly recreate the acoustics of the Albert Hall and weighs only a little more. Two skinheads compared the tattoos on their necks and an elderly wide-boy loaded televisions into a van. Joy drove away before anyone could steal his hubcaps.

'Now what?' I asked.

Flaherty's urbanity had driven off in the car with Joy. 'You're in no position to ask questions,' he told me, speaking quietly. 'You nearly fucked the whole operation. As it is we're going to have to change the timetable: I want you out of England quick, before you foul up any more.'

He led me to an anonymous door between an Italian café and a Pakistani newsagent, and knocked twice before continuing to be nasty to me. 'You've cost us a lot of effort and money. You can stay here until we get the flights rearranged. And don't even think of being clever: you're not up to it. We're only using you because we've got no one else.'

'You've got my dad,' I pointed out, peevishly. 'Which is why you can use me at all.'

Flaherty was unperturbed. Or at least, any perturbation he suffered came from a different source. 'Pete Joy isn't cheap,' he said, as peevish as I. 'The cause can do without solicitors' bills.' The door was opened by a large man in a green parka. Flaherty bundled me into a narrow stairway.

'I thought Joy was a radical,' I said to Flaherty over my shoulder, as we climbed the stairs.

'Radicals are more expensive than straight lawyers, but only a radical would handle this case at such short notice. Joy believes in the end of oppression in Ireland.' He would also believe in the end of capitalism, colonialism, exploitation, white flour and vivisection, if I knew anything. Flaherty appeared to have forgotten our cross words of a moment before, because he now spoke in a more amiable tone. 'He told me the police were part of a conspiracy of money aimed at the suppression of the working people. That's why he doesn't mind bribing them. He told me he was fighting capital with capital. He told me a lot, and it was all bullshit.'

The man in the parka opened a door at the top of the stairs. The door had been primed but never painted, and was formidably thick. I was let in; Flaherty followed. The parka stayed on the landing.

'You're here till you leave for Greece. You'll be seeing no one, contacting no one.' He cocked his head towards the parka. 'I've got a bloke watching you day and night, just in case you pull any other crackpot tricks.'

I looked round the room. It was a small apartment, about the size of a standard fitted wardrobe. I know about fitted wardrobes: I've hidden in more than one. The biggest difference was the decor. In a fitted wardrobe there is always something – a fur, a feather boa – that makes you sneeze the moment after some hulking male voice has announced, 'Hello darling, I forgot my keys/

the meeting was cancelled/the car broke down in Dulwich.' In Flaherty's safe house there was nothing, and then more nothing, and then a mattress on the floor and an ancient Christmas tree propped against the wall above a rug of beige pine needles.

'How long am I going to be here?' I asked.

'Until we can get your trip to Greece reorganized.'

'And how long's that likely to be?' I knew a man once who wrote a play about two penniless characters queuing outside the only working cubicle in a public lavatory. It was very profound. The public convenience was a metaphor for twentieth-century Britain, and the characters kept asking one another questions like 'Why are we here?' and 'What's it all about?'. So did the audience, and I only bring the dreary subject up at all because I used to believe that play to be the most tedious experience in the western hemisphere; faced with the prospect of a week in Flaherty's safe house, even *Waiting for the Toilet* seemed to have its moments.

I guess Flaherty recognized my misgivings. 'You can read in the bog,' he told me. 'You should be grateful we need you. I've had enough trouble just persuading some of the fellers not to kneecap you.' He went to the door, and the man in the parka stood aside to let him out.

'Thanks,' I called after him. 'Anyone would think it was my fault I ended up at the police station.'

Flaherty turned at the top of the stairs and looked at me. 'And whose fault was it if it wasn't yours?' he asked, then left.

'Bye-bye!' I shouted. He ignored me. The parka slammed the door and I was alone.

I had a look round. The windows had been covered with sheets of brown paper, but there were enough gaps for me to see the street beyond. The street was as uninspiring as the room. A door led to the bathroom. It had been recently converted and not quite completed. A floorboard was still misplaced, revealing a couple of plastic pipes beneath. There were strips of paper saying 'Please remove before using' round the seat of the bog. I read them while I had a pee: it was about all there was to read.

There wasn't much reading matter in the other room either, just a 1978 copy of the *Sun* which had been used to block a hole in the skirting board. The mice had eaten page three. I went over to the Christmas tree. One bauble, untarnished and alien, still hung from its branches. I looked beyond its bright surface and saw myself reflected as a set of caricatures. With my head down, my eyes expanded, and the bags and the bruises round them, I looked like the late Marty Feldman. If I faced the bauble straight my nose grew as the rest of my features receded, so I looked like Pete Townshend of The Who. With my head up, my upper lip and mouth dominated and I looked like a white Frank Bruno. I looked like all of these people and none of them looked like me. I wanted to go home. Things could have been worse. I could have been cemented into the foundations of an M25 slip road. But, believe me, at the time it all seemed bad enough.

The days passed, eventually. Twice a day the parka came in with a take-away pizza in a big white box. It was all I ever got to eat, and he was the only person I saw. He rarely spoke, and when he did he revealed a mouth like a urinal wall, all chipped enamel and filthy words. I was surprised by his accent: he was a Londoner. 'How long are they keeping me here?' I asked.

'Fuck knows. Nothing to do with me, mate.'

'Oh.'

One day I caught him in a loquacious mood: he actually told me it was raining. 'Fucking raining', in fact. I already knew it was raining: I could hear it hitting the panes behind the brown paper. But I was hardly going to discourage this sort of communication.

'Is it really?'

'Yeah.'

'A lot?'

'Yeah.'

This was a real break-through. This was Conversation. Unfortunately, at that moment he had to leave.

The best day of all, however, was when he brought me a newspaper. It was the most wonderful present I've been given since my da gave me a George Best Manchester United jersey for my fifteenth birthday. I read it from cover to cover.

The world was coping with my absence well, and nothing much had changed. Teachers were complaining about pay. Arsenal had lost at home to Oxford. The Croupier Group was putting in a bid for some electronics company despite competition from abroad. The price of petrol was coming down. The EEC had failed to agree on a reform of the Common Agricultural Policy. The American hostages held in Qafadya were still there. I read these stories so often I memorized them, and then I memorized the adverts as well. I was just learning to recite that day's TV programmes too when, after a fortnight that had lasted twenty years, Flaherty visited.

'Time to be going to the airport,' he told me, and in a daze I followed him.

It was a fine spring night outside. He led me out to a car, my car, and sat me in the passenger seat. A heavy was driving, and my luggage, packed for me, was in the back. 'Have a good trip,' said Flaherty. 'And it was nice of you to give us the car.'

I thought he was borrowing it; he made me feel I had bequeathed it to him. I was going to miss my car, my dear old Astra; I'd worked hard for it – *per ardua ad Astra* – and we'd been through a lot together. Two clutches, five tyres, a new piston rod and a hedge, to be precise.

I was going to miss the plane too if the heavy didn't put his foot down. I was due to check in at 3.15 am; my service-station digital said it was 2.16, which could have meant anything. April had become early May while I'd been reading the lurid details of 'Vicar Involved In Drug Ring Vice' for the seventy-third time. A full moon looked down from a cloudless sky. It was good to be in the open again. The pylons waved at me through the moonlight. The trunk road headed for Greece. And the heavy drove like a drain.

We were twenty minutes late. You can tell I'm not familiar with international travel; I thought I'd have missed my plane. Instead, after checking in I discovered my plane was delayed in Bologna and that I had two and a half hours to play with. I did the usual things: watched a couple of boring planes refuel beneath the arc-lights, wondered where on earth all these people could be going, went to the duty-free shop and exceeded the credit limit on my Excess card, drank too many cups of plastic coffee, became a seasoned traveller who laughed at the consternation of the new arrivals when they learned that their planes were held up. I was just impressing a pretty American with acute observations of Thai customs I'd read in a copy of *National Geographic* last time I'd visited the VD clinic when my flight was called. 'I must go,' I told her. 'My editor needs the Thessalonika story bad and I could do with the break after covering the Philippines for *Time*.' All right, so it was bull, but would she have believed the truth?

Departure Gate 19, it said on the boarding pass. It was a long walk. Halfway to Thessalonika I joined another queue. Do they do time-and-motion studies any more? A time-and-motion study of an airport would discover a hell of a lot of time and damn all motion. I remarked as much to the man standing next to me, an overweight Londoner with an overweight camera jutting from his navel. 'Yuh,' was all he said in reply.

I thought this was the end of the conversation, but apparently the Cockney considered this brief exchange the equivalent of slitting our wrists and mingling blood. I heard about his mother, who was half Jewish, and his father, who ran a minicab service from Hackney and was doing nicely thank you, and his sister the dancer, not to be confused with his other sister who'd married some bloke from Sheffield, and how he was breaking into promotional work, whatever that was, through some mates in the print trade, and had I ever been to Balham, he was buying a little place, you'll have seen it if you know it, about halfway along the High Street above a launderette, convenient for the video shop, and I nodded and smiled and dreamed of safe houses in Camden.

Meanwhile the corridor filled with returning holidaymakers wearing their holiday clothes, all nipples and proud gooseflesh and long brown legs turning blue. I smiled at some of the lovelier ones but they didn't smile back: I was too pale for their newly acquired tans.

At last we boarded. My Cockney buddy was sitting half an aisle away, which proves there is a God, and I had a seat between a harassed mother and the window. I looked out. Dawn was on its way. The sky to the east was streaky with sunrise, the sky to the north full of London's glow. We taxied away from the buildings, turned in a wide arc and accelerated.

I'm not that fond of flying, myself. I don't like the cramped seats, the lousy food, the boring view of the top of the clouds, the five miles between me and the ground. We took off. Below us the lights on the cars and the houses became fake stars that couldn't keep up, while above us were real stars that could. Just like Hollywood, I guess. As we climbed, so did the sun, dawning at double speed as the horizon moved away, glinting on our wings.

Air-hostesses, like nurses, are never as pretty as you'd like them to be, but I'll always be fond of women who bring round cheap booze. The first double tasted good. It didn't get rid of the feeling that I was five miles up, but it did taste good. The second tasted even better. By the fourth the sensation of flying had gone; by the sixth it had returned, and who needed an aeroplane?

It was my first drink for a week. It seeped into my organs, lubricating them. My brain pulled up an armchair and lit a cigarette. My heart started to read a good book. Only my liver, the old killjoy, complained, and my brain, dozing in front of an open fire, ignored it.

When I woke we were landing. Sunlight shimmered outside. I saw a blue armoured car marked POLICE patrolling the tarmac, and lots of armed soldiers standing round our plane. Oh, shit. I wasn't much encouraged by the large sign above the airport building either: a circle with a line through it, an E, two more Es in a different style, a sort of A, a different A without a line through it, an O, an N, an I, a K and another I. Oeeeaaoniki? Where was I? Hawaii?

Still, there didn't seem much choice about getting off. Everyone else was at it, bustling in the corridors and grabbing their bags. The book Flaherty had given me was in my hand luggage. I looked out of the window again. The soldiers looked back and chewed their gum in unison. I slipped the book from my bag and left it on the seat. Relieved, I followed the others.

The soldiers watched us walk across the apron. Their unfriendly foreign stares burned holes behind my ears. Still, at least I was clean; at least there would be nothing except suspicion to pin on me. The heavy heat first cleared and then fuddled the booze in my head. I staggered slightly and had to pretend I had tripped, cursing an imaginary obstacle for the benefit of my fellow travellers. They did not look impressed; they looked like they thought I was drunk. Bugger them, I decided: I may be drunk but I'm all right. I'm clean. I'm clean because Flaherty said so. Flaherty's big in the INLA. Flaherty's big everywhere. So up yours you disapproving matrons, up yours you stupid Balkan soldiery. Call yourselves soldiers anyway, I thought, with a perverse patriotism. Come off it. I've chucked bricks at the Grenadier Guards, shouted rude words at the Black Watch; the British soldier is the best in the world.

We reached passport control. I felt blithe and cocky, confident of my passport, confident of myself. Then the woman I'd sat next to on the plane handed me back my book.

FOUR

My brain felt like it was wrestling in mud, and the mud was being trodden down to my bowels. Actually, this pressure on my rectum helped matters: I wasn't sure where I was or what I was doing, but at least I knew where I wanted to go. A large sign said TOILET in nine European languages on the far wall of the building. Ah, blessed relief, I thought, until I realized the toilets were the far side of passport control.

The airport was a flat unsympathetic building, a cross between the dining hall in a modern school and the cold store of a disused abattoir. The floors were tiled and polished and the bright lights were all strip and no tease. Partitioning the room was passport control, a broken line of grey boxes like a barricade. It was patrolled by grim men who pretended their uniforms hid compassion and humanity. The pretence didn't work.

We were herded towards the conveyor belt that delivered our luggage. I didn't have much and didn't have long to wait; I saw my Cockney pal struggling with more bags than I had socks and wondered who'd got it wrong, him or me. While I waited for the rest of the party, caught between the urge to get to the bog and the urge to remain just where I was, unarrested, I looked quickly through the book I'd been given.

I hadn't dared open it before. Having opened it I was none the wiser. It was called *Advanced Mathematical Tables* and seemed to consist of three hundred pages of numbers and columns. At the beginning were various formulae; after that it was all tables. Not exactly holiday reading maybe, but definitely and reassuringly respectable. The pressure on my bowels eased.

It eased even more when I got through the customs check. I'd have thought that my passport photo alone would have been cause for suspicion: it was an old, hairy one that made me look like a member of the PLO. But then everyone's passport makes them look like Yasser Arafat or Myra Hindley, and I was passed through without a murmur. Bang went the stamp on an empty page. I was legitimate.

I hurried to the toilet and relieved another cause for anxiety, which only left twelve thousand, three hundred and ten others. Whatever was going to go wrong hadn't gone wrong yet, but there was plenty of time. I returned to the foyer.

My tour party was already outside, lining up for the coach; the courier was allocating resorts and hotels. 'Where am I?' I asked.

'The last resort,' she replied. It figured.

Flaherty had told me I would meet my contact at the airport, so I looked round for him. He'll have to be quick, I reasoned, because soon I'll be on a bus: perhaps he won't turn up at all, which would suit me. But then the courier drew me to one side. 'Here's the ticket to Rome and the address,' she said in a slight Belfast burr. 'You must memorize the address and destroy the paper.'

'It's just like James Bond,' I told her. 'Should I eat it?'

She ignored me. 'You've missed the plane you should've been on,' she said, as if it was my fault.

'Our plane was delayed in Bologna,' I explained in defence.

'Well, you'll have to wait till tomorrow now. The next plane leaves at 7.30. Be sure not to miss this one.'

'Where shall I sleep?' I asked. It was not an innocent question: the courier was an attractive lass, and I wondered whether, as a supporter of the cause, she might be willing to make the penultimate sacrifice for one about to make the ultimate.

She wasn't. 'In the airport. Have you got a blanket?'

'No.'

'Oh well. You probably won't need one. Bye.'

And with that she went.

Greek time was two hours ahead; my service-station watch said it was 12.17, but a clock on the wall said 9.30. I wondered about putting my watch right, a complicated manoeuvre requiring a ballpoint pen, plenty of patience and three hands, but decided against it. I was only going to be in Greece a day.

This decision meant that I'd have to find something else to occupy myself, so I checked the time of my flight on a multilingual board and discovered it didn't exist. I could go to Paris, Frankfurt, Munich, London, Athens or Sarajevo, but not, apparently, to Rome. I thought maybe this would be the expected cock-up, but it wasn't. A hairy young man at the enquiry desk told me that the 7.30 flight was to Athens, where I was to make a connection. Fair enough: now I only had twenty-one and a half hours to kill.

I watched a few planes fly in and a few planes fly out. The soldiers and the armoured car milled around dejectedly: the soldiers looked as bored as I was. I decided to walk to Thessalonika. Like most airports this one was outside the town, but I could see the tower blocks in the distance, silhouetted in front of high wooded hills that looked like they'd been carved from the sponge used for making flower arrangements. The walk took maybe an hour. The day was hot and dusty. I found a taverna in a square and ordered coffee. When it arrived it was cold, iced, and splendid. Suddenly life looked up.

I hung around the town all day. It was a bigger place than I had expected, with a port and lots of high buildings. I walked down wide avenues and decided it was time to eat. After a while I found a bar that looked interesting and took my credit card. The menu was in two columns. One was in Greek and the other wasn't: the second column said things like 'Pork chips' and 'Grilled lion'. The waiter came and I pointed. Everything I pointed at seemed to be off. Eventually I shrugged and ordered a beer, and he came back with a large salad of sour cheese, cucumbers, tomatoes, olives and olive oil. Mostly olive oil. I began to understand why the Greeks are so brown: it's not just the sun; they're basted in oil.

I tried ordering beer again, with more success. The beer was cold and sharp and German: it went down well. I had another and then one or two more and settled my bill, which nearly caused a diplomatic incident. In time though I signed, keeping the sliver of greaseproof paper as a receipt, and went out into the heat. The streets were full of dust and sunlight and cars, the dust turning autumnally among the exhaust fumes where the sun caught it, and the cars honking pointlessly in the traffic jams. An ambulance went by. It squirted red light like a severed artery, but had a low, almost silent siren: it was the quietest thing on the road. I wandered around: I saw a museum full of relics of Alexander the Great's dad, and any number of fancy churches, and drank iced coffee and chilled beer. I was in such a good mood I even offered a silent toast to Flaherty, raising my glass to the sun. But all things must end, and even the Grecian sun sets: I began to feel hungry again.

I couldn't find the bar I'd been to before, but there was no shortage of places to eat. These places had a strong family likeness anyway: plastic awnings, cheap cutlery, bilingual menus, the faint stench of drains. The menu seemed identical to the last one I'd looked at. They were standard, I worked out, and only the food with the price pencilled against it was available. Right. I ordered moussaka and chips and went over to the juke box. Facing it and making a selection was a man I thought I knew from earlier in the day. He had stood beside me at the Philip of Macedon museum. I recognized his harelip. His white suit, slightly grubby at the collar and cuffs, gave him a dated, beachcomber look. He looked out of place at the jukebox, but he smiled at me when I approached. 'English?' I asked.

Instead of speaking he put a finger to his lips, mysteriously. I repeated my question. He smiled, then left the taverna without hearing his tunes. I wasted some time wondering who he was, and then accepted that mystery was mandatory in anything Flaherty arranged. I wondered whose side he was on: I got to know him better later, but I never did learn that.

The bar was comfortable and the music good. The jukebox was sleek and modern, with the song titles arranged in columns like packets in a cigarette machine. The titles were all in English, which was fair enough because so were the songs, and hiding among the Woodbines and Park Drives was a column marked Golden Oldies. I selected the Crystals, 'Da Doo Ron Ron', and sat down, half-expecting harelip to return.

As the light faded the place got busy. Younger customers replaced my song with pop pap. I drank a bottle of appalling red wine. It was a good place to be, I felt, and buoyed by the booze I began to enjoy myself. More customers arrived, filling the place with cigarette smoke and designer clothes. Everyone seemed to know everyone else: these were masculine groups, with attendant women, and the men seemed intent on pleasure. That was fine by me.

Some of the revellers spoke English and, like many drunks with command of a foreign language, were showing off. 'You come from England? No?'

'From London,' I said. They'd understand that.

'Ah! London. I go to study in London maybe one year, maybe two.'

'That's very nice. What are you doing now?'

'Eh?'

'What do you do now? What is your job?'

'No job. Tomorrow we all are to join the army.'

'Oh.'

'We do not have choice, understand. Government says all young men join.'

'Ah. Conscription. I see.'

'You in army sometime?'

Does the Irish National Liberation Army count? That was a form of conscription too, in a way. 'Come on Jack, it's time we was making a man of you.' First we threw insults, then bricks, then grenades. The grenades were small, green, knobbled and packed with malice; they sat in your hand like bad-tempered brussels sprouts. My throwing arm was about as accurate as a weather forecast though, so they moved me on to mortars. I'm not sure why. The mortars were easy to carry but hard to aim: my score

was one police station (no casualties), one post office (no casualties
but I scared the hell out of the queuing pensioners, and me), and
one field (I was aiming for an army patrol near the border: I scored
one Friesian cow, two pheasants and a heap of unidentified bits
which might have been a middle-sized dog).

'I ask you, you in army sometime my friend?'

'No,' I answered. 'No. I was never in the army.'

'You want new drink?' asked my new friend.

Do bunnies bonk in burrows? 'Yes please.'

'I order one.' He called the barman over and spoke rapidly. It
was all Greek to me. A glass of water arrived, and a similar-sized
glass containing a thick brown liquid that looked like cognac and
smelt like a sweet shop.

'Ouzo?' I asked.

'Is good?'

'Very good,' I replied. The water turned the Ouzo to milk. I
knocked it back and waved for another. My companions were
impressed.

Northern Europeans seem to drink much more than those who
live by the Mediterranean. Perhaps we need the booze to keep out
the cold, or maybe it's a cultural thing to do with the pace of life:
a Greek can make a glass of beer last him an evening and no one's
going to chivy him; try that in Maida Vale. Watching my Irish thirst
at work seemed to give them genuine pleasure, so I indulged them,
and me. 'You want one more?' I was asked.

'I want a hell of a lot more than one,' I replied.

I could develop a liking for this stuff, I decided. Its sharp
sweetness peeled the nicotine off my teeth and the lining off my
stomach. Its watery whiteness reminded me of the mother's milk
I'd watched ooze in four pearls from my wife's nipple when she
fed our babies. Its taste was street corners in Derry, triangular
white bags of hard bronze aniseed balls, taunting the Prod kids
and scuffing our shoes. Like all good booze, I guess Ouzo is bottled
nostalgia.

I lost count of how many I'd drunk. The club closed. I tried to sign for my meal and my drinks but failed and someone else settled up for me. We walked outside, exchanging the close warmth of the club for the open warmth of the street. The sun was rising over the city, and I blearily recognized a man in a white suit, a man with a harelip who followed us along the street, but I was trying to teach my Greek friends a Republican ballad and was buggered if I could remember the words, so harelip was low on my priorities.

We got into cars, setting off in a convoy out of the town. I vaguely remember the white suit standing in the street watching us drive away, and one of the Greeks asking if I knew him, but I answered 'No', which was more or less true, and then we were round a corner. The night was dark, and then not so dark. We drove up the hills, away from the city. They had a go at teaching me one of their songs, and laughed wildly at my mistakes. The increasing light revealed a road that wound dangerously round the hills, loose-fitting and temporary as a scarf. Lining the roadside at irregular intervals were little shrines, roofed like birdhouses, with crosses and icons inside.

The girl sitting next to me spoke good English. 'The shrines are given by those who have survived accidents at the spot,' she said. 'To say thank you they were not killed.'

There were shrines all along that road, except on the sharpest bends. No one survives the accidents there, I guess.

I got my standard alcohol lust, the one that starts at the end of your prick and makes you wonder if you need a pee, and then slowly moves back into your groin, hardening you as it goes. I put a hand on the girl's knee. She didn't object. I slipped it beneath the hem of her dress, tantalizing her thighs with my stretched little finger. She stiffened a little but let me keep it there.

Temporal love is one thing, spiritual love quite another, and I had drunk plenty of spirits that night. My soul reached out for this girl, and so did my fingers, pussyfooting towards her pussy. I've always been a child at heart; I just love going back to the womb. But then she hit me, hard, across the face, and that was the end of that.

You're probably thinking, and with justice, what a bastard I am to assault the poor girl in the first place, and I suppose in most ways you're right. On the other hand, if I hadn't dipped my finger she wouldn't have hit me, and if she hadn't hit me I wouldn't have sobered up nearly so fast, and if I hadn't sobered up I'd have missed my plane, which all goes to prove damn all.

I was only just able to persuade my joy-riding companions to get me to the airport on time. They were sobering up too by now, looking miserable and apprehensive. They didn't look like soldiers. But in Greece even the soldiers don't look like soldiers. I said goodbye, and the girl who'd been sitting next to me gave me a surprising and friendly kiss. Spiritual love is all very well, but temporal love takes time, and time I didn't have. It was a shame. I kissed her back, watched them drive away and, because the plane was delayed in Bologna, had plenty of time to go to the bog, have a wash and get changed.

I had another look at *Advanced Mathematical Tables* while I waited. It certainly looked innocent. But maybe it was a code book? Or maybe the formulae at the beginning were for making bombs. Nuclear bombs? I put the book away. 'What is knowledge but grieving?' the Earl of Lytton had written. Obviously he'd met Flaherty too. Then I looked at the address: 'Ria Mazzanati 287'. There was no way I'd remember that, so I tucked the paper in the book like a bookmark, and as I did so my flight was called. I walked across the warming tarmac; halfway across I remembered to look for the man with the harelip, and though I could not see him through the reflecting plate-glass airport windows I had a suspicion he was there.

The plane was small, a French-built Caravelle. I boarded it and found a window seat where I dutifully fastened my seatbelt. We waited in a rising roar of sound and then moved heavily down the runway, until the everyday impossible happened and the plane lifted off the ground.

There were no drinks served on the flight to Athens, which was maybe a good thing: I hadn't been sober since leaving Gatwick. I looked out of the window till I was browned off with brown hills and bored with the bordering sea, and then thought about sleeping, but it was only a forty-five minute flight and the plane was already dropping.

We came to land in Athens. Athens: now there's a place to make you really appreciate the genius of the Ancient Greeks. The Acropolis isn't just beautiful, it's also built on a hill. And let's be honest, if you're going to build something beautiful in Athens you'd want to build it on a hill. Because the rest of Athens stinks. Really stinks. Imagine being stuck in the dustbin of a Greek take-away off the Tottenham Court Road. Imagine being interred in a Greek waiter's Y-fronts. Imagine spending your days in the matronly armpit of a syphilitic Greek widow's sackcloth. And then imagine all that in the atmosphere of a busy multi-storey carpark above a sewage works. Add a temperature of 102 in the shade and maybe, just maybe, you'll catch on.

Apart from that, I'm sure Athens is very nice. And in all honesty I can't pretend to be an expert. I never even left the airport.

I was flying Attic Airways. The name was doubtless a reference to Greece's ancient past, but it put me in mind of climbing steep stairs to a load of old junk. I climbed the stairs anyway, and a stewardess dressed in pale-blue greeted me and indicated where I should sit.

The Rome plane was a jumbo jet, much bigger than either of the planes I had been on before, and it was half empty. I had a seat in the middle of the plane, well away from the token windows, and nothing to do. There was only one good-looking single woman on the flight, dark-skinned and dark-haired, and she wouldn't meet my eye. We all listened politely as the stewardess described the emergency exits. Then the plane taxied and roared and we took off, flying through hot Athenian air that was as lumpy as packet soup. The pretty lady stood up to check the luggage above her seat. She wore a blue silk blouse and blue jeans, and her bottom was worth a second look. When she sat down I noticed she had an interesting mole on the side of her throat. I offered her a smile like I might offer a cigarette, but she turned it down.

I guess I must have dozed, because the next thing I knew three gentlemen with guns were standing by the door to the cabin, ordering us to keep calm.

FIVE

The professionals were all very professional: the captain made a brief announcement in English, Greek and Italian to the effect that we had been hijacked, the stewardess tended the cases of hysteria, and the men with the guns watched from behind their dark glasses. We amateurs coped less well, and sat with open mouths and white faces, like the audience at a horror movie when the lights come up unexpectedly.

A fourth hijacker strolled through from the cockpit, leaving the door open behind him. He pulled the stewardess's microphone down and spoke to us in excellent American English. 'Ladies and gentlemen,' he said. 'Please do not panic; there is no cause for alarm. This plane has been commandeered by the freedom fighters of the Islamic Army for a Socialist Palestine. Please accept my apologies for any inconvenience caused.' He seemed very calm, but there was something exaggerated about his poise: I was reminded of Derrymen in cosy parlours, with their cigarettes burning and the curtains drawn, counting the time till the bombs went off.

The leader returned to the cockpit, and almost at once the plane banked to the left. The gunmen braced themselves against the seats but did not lower their guns. If they had emotions they were not letting on. Through the windows I saw the frayed coastline of Yugoslavia below us, and then the plane righted itself. It seemed we were heading south.

Until that moment hijack had been no more than a way people greeted me; now it was a fear that pulped my guts. I was not sure what I feared. My life had been pretty irrelevant to me for some time; it had been out of my control long before Flaherty turned

42

up. This was just another twist of fate. But I had never really doubted that I would survive before, and now, despite the reassuring words of the hijackers, I knew I would die. All I really wanted was to go home. This would remain my ambition for a long time. My ambition, my aim in life, my lot. Show me the way to go home.

The rest of the passengers felt the same, I guess. They whimpered and whispered and sweated just like me, and the sunglasses watched us without pity. A hint of nervousness on the gunmen's part might have done us all good, given us a chance to loosen our emotions. Instead we all pretended things were normal, which made the tension worse.

All Irishmen live in the past. It is our natural home. We live in the past because the present is shitty, and for me on that plane at that moment it was even shittier than usual. Was it that or the terrorists that made me remember so clearly the Spa Hotel, Dublin, in the winter of 1974, and Costello's call to arms?

I was eighteen, and my adolescence had been spent in the Troubles. I was eager. The IRA had declared a ceasefire on the Brits, which for Seamus Costello and many like him, like me, was an act of treachery. We wanted a Socialist Ireland, a Republic Ireland, a Catholic Ireland, an Ireland born of the bomb and the rifle. No one mentioned that Socialism and Catholicism didn't mix. Our hijackers were Islamic Socialists; I don't suppose Islam and Socialism mix either. I prayed to Mary and all the saints that our hijackers had more sense than we'd had. They were certainly better dressed.

From time to time the plane banked, showing us sea and sky and no division between. We were flying lower now. The leader of the hijackers returned to the microphone. 'Ladies and gentlemen,' he announced. 'We shall shortly be landing in Benghazi.'

I expected him to tell us to extinguish our cigarettes and fasten our seatbelts, but he didn't.

'Please do not try to rise from your seats, either now or when we have landed. Anyone who attempts to do so will most certainly be shot.'

His voice seemed less confident now; he had not needed to make threats before. Perhaps something had gone wrong? Perhaps the plane had less fuel than he needed? Perhaps we were being tailed by Israeli fighters? Perhaps . . . perhaps, perhaps, perhaps. I realized, with something like guilt, that I'd lost that sense of the ridiculous which had helped me survive ridiculous situations. Perhaps when we landed I might be able to laugh at the irony that had hijacked me, a terrorist myself. Perhaps I might be able to see the funny side of their devout belief in something not worth believing. But not now: not with God knows how many feet of nothing beneath me and a pair of blind eyes holding a gun to my head.

The leader exchanged a few words with his fellow terrorists and then returned to the pilots, while his companions walked towards the back of the plane. Suddenly a hijacker was brought down, felled by a large Italian who made a grab for the gun. Then the gun went off, impossibly loud, and the Italian was dead. There was a hubbub of noise, made woolly as our ears still echoed the shot.

'Shut up!' called the leader of the hijackers, returning impotently to the mike. 'Shut up!'

Now there was real panic in his voice. He said a number of things in Arabic and his companions moved back down the plane, where they covered us with their guns. We heard the leader's deep breaths amplified through the loudspeakers as he tried to recover his composure.

'That was extremely foolish,' he said at last. He gestured with his gun to a passenger near him, a middle-aged woman. 'Come here,' he said, the impersonal microphone voice addressing us all. 'At once!'

The woman spoke in a rush of Italian. She seemed to be protesting that she did not understand, but as she spoke she stood, which suggested she did.

'Here!' commanded the leader again. She moved a few paces towards him, and as she approached he grabbed her quickly and put the gun to her head. 'Ladies and gentlemen,' he said. 'There shall be no more foolishness. We are not barbarians, but neither are we sentimentalists. Our cause is too large, and too important, to be hampered by the stupidity of a few individuals. Let this be a lesson to you all.'

There was another deafening shot. The Italian lady remained in his arms, but half her head was missing. The man she had been with, her husband perhaps, stood in his seat, but the terrorist turned on him at once and aimed his gun. As he did so he let the woman drop, and she fell to the floor, leaving bits of her head on his well-laundered shirt.

The husband sagged too, wailed in hideous grief, and sank back into his seat.

The leader used the microphone again, but spoke Arabic, and then returned to the cockpit. We sat in the stunned echo of the two fatal shots, and tasted the bile in our throats. I have seen violence before and grown used to its presence – in England a man can prove his virility by discussing the WBA championships and making occasional comments about the barmaid's boobs, whereas in Belfast we were discussing gun-runs and knee-capping – but this was the most cold-blooded act I had known, and my blood too ran cold.

The landing was an anticlimax. It seemed almost natural, almost the sort of thing that happens in the world we had inhabited that morning, before the shots and the deaths and the change of course. But when we had landed, and when the engines had died, there was nothing natural about the silence.

The gunmen patrolled us. We could see the white tension of their trigger fingers beneath their brown skin, and the sweat that beaded the lines of their moustaches. The leader called something from the door of the cockpit and one of the gunmen went through to him.

The leader emerged. 'We are about to refuel.' He tried to recapture his earlier urbanity, but failed. 'You will please remain silent at all times. You will please remain in your seats. Thank you.'

Through the plane's inadequate windows I could see the airport and its concrete runways, bright and almost white in the sun. Benghazi is in Libya, and if American propaganda is to be believed then Libya sides with terrorists, but our hijackers did not seem at ease here. A tanker approached and disappeared from view, and the fuselage clanged to the sound of refuelling. I felt safer and calmer now we had landed, but 'safer' and 'calmer' are relative terms.

At last the tanks in the wings were full, and the tanker drove away. We waited, and waited some more, but nothing happened. My watch was as useless as ever, but outside were the short sharp shadows of noon. Time passed, though stubbornly and resentfully; the shadows began to move and my tense muscles began to relax, until the engines fired unexpectedly and I nearly coughed up my kidneys in fear.

We taxied, accelerated, and took off. I saw the vanishing town, large and white and unsympathetic, dipping below our wings, and then we were flying over the sea. The plane turned back at once and we were over land again, an inhospitable land like an orange fog. Perhaps it was a sandstorm; perhaps it was the desert reflecting off the clouds. Whatever it was it terrified me, and it went on for ever beneath us.

Our flight went on for ever too. For ever and a day. The world was reduced to basics, to the burring, boring note of the engines, to the churning orange below, to the brilliant blue sky above. The terrorist leader seemed to have stopped giving us bulletins. He stayed with the pilot, as did one of his men. A Greek girl exchanged a tentative smile with one of the hijackers, but between their smiles was his gun. The pretty dark lady with the mole sat calmly, studying the headrest of the seat in front. I rested a hand on my knee and felt dampness. The hand explored my groin. Without much surprise I found I had wet myself, though I could not remember when. It did not seem to matter. The two bodies stayed where they had fallen.

The plane banked unexpectedly, and began to circle down. The descent could be measured in the pressure on our ears. The sign came on, telling us to fasten our seatbelts; I obeyed automatically. Below, as we banked, I saw an airstrip, a darker line on the sand. The airstrip was being swept by orange-white waves; the waves grew bigger as we came down, only to disappear as the horizon reared up.

There were a few buildings alongside the airstrip, a couple of parked vehicles, and beyond them high dunes. We swept by them all. The wheels touched and lifted, as though the sun-seared runway was too hot. Then we touched down again, more firmly, though we still careered wildly. There was the banshee sound as the engines were plunged into reverse, but no appreciable deceleration. We started to judder unpleasantly. I was aware that we were beginning to turn. The squeal of the wheels could be heard even over the engines as they tried defiantly to bring us round. I took tight hold of the arms of my seat and willed the plane to a halt. There was a lurch. We tilted and heard a new sound. Through the windows I saw the tip of a wing. It hit the ground, ripped and crumpled in an arc of sparks and leaping flames.

We were heading in a new direction now, towards the dunes. Flames and smoke licked what was left of the wing. Then the undercarriage on the other side must have given way, because there was another lurch, more profound than the first, and a piercing howl as we scraped the ground. We were spinning towards the dunes, squealing and burning and turning until, with a crash that drove the light from my eyes, we came to a violent stop.

When I could move and look up, the light seemed different. At first I thought the electricity had failed, but the effect was more peculiar than that. The fuselage was tilted up towards the nose: the front was in darkness, but the rear was still lit through the windows. I shook my head. Around me, there were sounds of shock and pain. A man was crying hysterically. A small boy was screaming. I looked out of the window and saw enough to realize that we were half-buried in sand. The wings had disappeared into the dune, which seemed to have extinguished the flames. The nose was buried deeper. I looked forward along the aisle. In the darkness I saw, coming through the pilots' door, a deep stream of white sand still moving, and thrust from the sand, the gun still clenched tight, was a hand in a well-laundered shirt. In the arid desert he'd drowned.

Six

God may know how long we waited, though there hadn't been much evidence of His presence recently; certainly I lost track of time. It probably wasn't a long wait because I had only just become aware of the heat in the cabin when the doors were opened and a new heat came in. Greece had been hot but this was different. This was a heat with no moisture, carried on a breeze that had never blown through a tree.

The stewardess had opened the door but a gunman ushered us out, while his companions made their way to the butchered nose of the plane. Unbelievably, no one in the body of the plane seemed much hurt: the dune must have absorbed our crash and the cabin crew had been smothered by the sand rather than crushed by the impact. We found ourselves maybe twenty feet from the ground when we got to the door. Looking forward, I could see how the plane had impaled the dune and up-ended slightly; looking back I could see dark marks leading from the runway to where we had finished, though whether the heat that shimmered above these marks came from still-burning petrol or the blaze of the sun I could not say. One by one, like parachutists, we were made to jump from the plane, each waiting until the one before had waded out of the knee-deep, impact-absorbing sand.

When I landed the sand was hideously hot. It climbed up my trouser legs and into the sleeves of my summer shirt. By the time I had stumbled out, the front of my trousers, once embarrassingly wet, was quite dry. From a long way off, a vehicle approached. The heat made it dance a shimmy and made the runway glisten like water. It seemed to be a long time coming, and then suddenly it stopped being a wraith and became a Land Rover, and half a dozen men in Arab clothes, armed with automatic rifles, stepped out and pointed their guns. They spoke to us in Arabic, and then in French, but they needn't have spoken at all. The gestures they made with their weapons said 'This way' in any language.

To begin with we thought we were rescued, but the embraces these new gunmen gave to the hijackers soon put paid to that hope. We were divided into groups of eight, and the guns told us to sit. There was no shade and the sun was unbearable. Meanwhile, as the first group was herded into the Land Rover, the rest of us had our pockets emptied.

I didn't have much on me. In my wallet there were thirty drachmas in notes, my driving licence, and assorted bits of plastic: my cheque card, my Sparkycard and Excess card, my kidney donor card, my library card and my phonecard. None of these seemed to interest them much, which, unless they'd been planning to order a book on renal surgery by phone, was hardly surprising. But I also had my British passport, and that did grab their attention. It was attention I could have done without, though at least when they stood over me they gave me some shade. Already my skin, barely browned by a day in Greece, was turning a fierce red wherever it was exposed, and my bottom was being fried through my lightweight trousers.

When the Land Rover returned I was singled out and led to it. They sat me in the back, alone. The metal seats, even inside, were scorchingly hot, but the canvas hood sheltered me from the direct blaze. I was horrified to find my mouth entirely dry, and my tongue already swollen. If this was what an hour in the desert did, how did people survive a lifetime?

I'd expected to be driven off at once – the Land Rover couldn't hold many and if they wanted to ferry all the passengers they'd have to make a dozen trips – but instead we waited. Unwanted visions of iced coffee and chilled German beer popped into my head like prices in an old-fashioned cash-register. I must have been sun-struck: I remember trying to whistle 'Why Are We Waiting', only to discover that my dry lips could make no sound.

At last an Arab with a black front tooth looked in on me. He said something in Arabic, a language which always sounds contemptuous and this time probably was, and spat drily into the truck. Then some of his companions appeared, carrying the corpse of the hijackers' leader. They shoved it, rather awkwardly, into the back with me. The corpse was undamaged though stiff, and was matted with flies.

There was another wait, a chance for me to get acquainted with the corpse, and then the pretty lady with the mole was gestured in at gunpoint. I tried to smile, maybe share a little companionship, but my heart wasn't in it and neither was hers. The Land Rover pulled away.

Behind us, though we travelled fast, we could still see the high tail of the plane through the back of the truck and the swirling disturbed flies, and then it had disappeared into the heat haze that shimmered away all horizons. No one sat in the back to guard us; there was no escape in the desert and they knew it.

At least the journey gave me time to think, despite the flies. I made a try at summing up my situation. Assuming my British passport, which they had taken from me, was the reason I had been selected to ride shotgun in this hearse, then if I could explain to them that I was Catholic-Irish I might be all right. But would they know what Catholic-Irish meant, or care? After all, Shi'ite was a word I used when I missed a bus; why should they understand the complexities of Irish politics? I didn't. What I needed was proof that I was a freedom fighter like them; that way they might be sympathetic. But what proof? The only thing I had was the book Flaherty had given me, and that was impenetrably innocent, surely. Besides, it was still on the plane.

We reached the buildings we had passed before. The return journey seemed to have taken a long time, which showed how fast the plane had been going when it landed. A couple of Arabs came to the back of the truck and opened the gate. I stood to get out but they ignored me and ushered my dark lady down. Then black-tooth appeared, spat again and waved me from the truck.

He seemed to like talking to me, because he kept up a running commentary of throaty noises as he led me to the simple white buildings; every so often I replied in my politest voice and told him to fuck off. He didn't seem to mind, but then he was probably saying the same to me.

The building he took me to was more dilapidated than it had seemed from a distance. The door was a sheet of corrugated iron and the interior was full of sand. The pretty lady from the plane seemed to have vanished; the only furniture was an old white chair. Black-tooth sat on the floor, and after a while so did I. A few of the Arabs meandered about, but they soon tired of that and wandered off, leaving me alone with black-tooth's invigorating conversation. I ran through my Arab vocabulary – yashmak, bazaar, fez – which whiled away almost a moment, and then my mind was exhausted. At last the door was pushed aside. The doorway was a rectangle of brilliance in the wall, and a tall figure was silhouetted against it.

The newcomer walked in. He was rather nattily dressed in a white linen suit, with a pale-yellow tie round his neck and a checkered napkin bound by a braid round his head. Black-tooth did not stand as this man walked in, but he did look subdued and I guessed that the stranger was an important man.

A few words of Arabic were exchanged before the man in the suit spoke to me. 'So, you are an imperialist shit,' he announced pleasantly.

'I'm Irish,' I replied.

'Really? Then why have you a British passport, please?'

'Northern Irish,' I told him. 'From Derry . . . Londonderry.'

'I do not think this is relevant. You carry a British passport. The crimes of the British against the Arab peoples are legion. Moreover, Britain today is a lackey of the United States. The United States defends Israel and bombs Libya. Despite our little border problem with Libya they are our fraternal Islamic neighbours. Ergo, you, imperialist shit, are an enemy.' His accent was curious and harsh. It reminded me a little of the way South Africans speak.

'I most assuredly am not,' I said, and I noticed how some reflex had flushed my Ulster accent out of my past. 'I'm a God-fearing Irish Republican and I'm as opposed to Britain as a man can decently get.' The dryness in my throat seemed to suit this accent.

'A Republican?'

'A nationalist. A terrorist. Like you.'

'I am not a terrorist,' said the man primly. 'I am a soldier. You are of the IRA?'

I wondered about saying 'Yes' but decided against it. 'The INLA,' I said. 'You've heard of it?'

My interrogator suddenly squatted just in front of me. He had a handsome thin face and dark penetrating eyes. He aimed these eyes straight at mine. 'You have just bought yourself a little time,' he said. 'If you can convince me you are telling the truth you will live. If you have lied to me you will die.'

My mouth couldn't get any drier, but that didn't stop it trying. 'I'm in the INLA,' I insisted.

'Anyone could say that.' Unexpectedly he offered me a cigarette, a French one from a pale-blue packet, and I took it. 'Prove it,' he said.

I let him light the cigarette for me. My hands were shaking as I took it from my mouth, and its dryness tugged at my lip. 'I'm on an INLA mission now,' I said.

'Really? Doing what?' His curiosity was no more than polite.

'A delivery job.' I was talking fast now. 'I was taking a book from London to Rome . . .'

'The flight we commandeered was from Athens to Rome.'

'I was sent to Thessalonika first, rather than straight to Rome.'

'Why?'

I paused. 'I don't know. To shake off suspicion, I suppose. I had to write fourteen postcards which would be posted from Greece while I was away.' The man nodded and I continued. 'I went from London to Thessalonika where I was given a ticket to Athens, and another from Athens to Rome . . . That's all I know.'

'And this book you were taking? Why?'

'I don't know . . .' Suddenly I remembered. 'It's to do with the Cairo Accord.'

Suddenly he sprang from his heels and stood. 'The Cairo Accord!'

'That's right.'

'You know about the Cairo Accord?'

Well, obviously I did, but I was in no position to tell him he was asking daft questions. 'Yes.'

'Then you have lied to me.'

'Eh?' I thought I'd just proved I was telling the truth.

'You gave me the impression you were a mere messenger boy. If you know about the Cairo Accord you must be much more than that.' He smiled. 'Of course, I understand that you had to be devious. I admire the way you hid your stature with your talk of "being sent" and "being told".' He held out a hand and pulled me to my feet, where he embraced me. Under the circumstances, this seemed to be a Good Thing, so I embraced him back. 'Allow me to introduce myself: Mohammed al Fahd ould Ely ould Ahkmed, Major of the Patriotic Qafadyan Armed Forces, Intelligence Division.'

'I'm Jack Diamond,' I said, and he embraced me again.

'I am very pleased to meet you, Mr Diamond. Or is it Mr? You have a rank?'

'No, no rank.'

'As you wish.' He took me by the hand and led me back to the blistering sunlight of the desert. I felt oddly coy, standing there holding hands with him like we were courting, but it was an improvement on having guns pointed at me. 'You're welcome to Qafadya,' he said, gesturing with his free arm.

Away from the superheated concrete runway, where the light was as warped as a politician's reasoning, the air was clear, showing me a vast nothing. You're welcome to Qafadya, believe me. Until then I had thought of Nature as something green and growing, but nature in the desert was different. It was on the side of the town planners, the carpark builders, the men whose idea of progress is to tear down trees and replace them with concrete. I looked at a spasmodic lizard scuttling along the sand, and a solitary tree that squatted between me and the horizon, and was awed and horrified and afraid.

Still, at least it was tidy.

'We must get you to Djarouane,' said the major. 'Have you everything you need for the conference?'

'I left everything in the plane,' I admitted, while I wondered what conference he meant. Flaherty hadn't mentioned it.

'That is unfortunate, though I suppose any other action would have seemed suspicious. We shall go back for your belongings.'

We returned to the Land Rover. The dead leader's body had been removed, and lay a discreet distance away, the face covered by his head cloth. In another Land Rover, parked by the back of the buildings, was the lady with the mole. I waved, hoping my new friendship with our kidnappers would comfort her, but she looked stonily past me.

The major climbed in the back with me; a minion handed him a big blue plastic picnic box, the sort that keeps things cool.

'Would you like a drink?' he asked as we set off back to the plane.

This is the most unnecessary question in the Diamond lexicon. Do I ever not want a drink? Mind you, normally I like a bit of spirit to what I pour down my throat; normally a bottle of tepid Coke would be a long way short of fitting the bill. But not then, and that Coke was the best, most intoxicating, most wonderful drink I can recall – though admittedly there have been some pretty wonderful drinks I can't recall.

Most of the passengers were lying down when we arrived, and few of them bothered to look up. With no shade and unsuitable clothes, they were suffering in the sun. 'We must retrieve your documents,' announced the major. We climbed up a mound of sand that burnt like the clap and entered the cabin by the forward door. The major's men had excavated the bodies of the crew and the hijack victims and piled them by the door. Swarming around them were a million small black flies. I wondered what the flies had lived on before we arrived; perhaps, like the major, they had been told of our coming in advance.

My hand luggage, a plastic bag marked 'Duty Free', was more or less where I'd left it on the floor by my seat, though the crash had spread things about: empty crisp packets, a few ring pulls, and a long till-roll receipt that detailed things I couldn't remember buying. My other bag, with my clothes and the book, had been in an overhead luggage locker, but the crash had forced this open and the bag was on a neighbouring seat. It was lucky the plane had been half-empty; *Advanced Mathematical Tables* was a heavy book by any standards and would have brained whoever it hit. I sorted through my possessions to make sure the book was still there; the major searched through the bag, still looking for weapons I suppose, and then the two of us returned to his vehicle. Another Land Rover had arrived, and another group of passengers was being escorted to it. Of the remaining few, those who bothered to look up did so with listless eyes. I saw blisters appearing on their faces, and their lips were turning grey.

'The passengers need water,' I told the major.

'I can do nothing for them,' he replied. 'Officially they are not here. Officially I am not here. They are hostages of the Islamic Army of Palestine, who have landed at a secret and unknown destination in the Sahara. The machinations of imperialist western nations have deprived the Qafadya air force of effective radar, which means there is no way we can trace a low-flying aeroplane over the desert. Attic Airways Flight KP187 has vanished, and informally the officers of the Patriotic Qafadyan Armed Forces will tell any newsman interested that it is probably in Libya, though officially of course we would never betray an ally like that. After all, we would not want the American F-111s to bomb our loyal Islamic neighbour again now, would we? Even though there is that little border dispute between our two countries. On the other hand, the hostages we already hold in the American embassy in Bahir have made us unpopular: we do not want to provoke the United States further or they may bomb us.'

I had forgotten about the American hostages in Qafadya. 'So where will the new hostages be kept?' I asked.

The major looked around him. Except for the rolling dunes to the north, the landscape was as flat as an amateur recital of *The Desert Song*. 'There is plenty of room here,' said the major, his voice equally flat. 'And now I must take you to Djarouane, which is the regional capital of Saharan Qafadya. From there you can travel to Bahir, and from Bahir you can get a plane to Rome. The Patriotic Qafadyan Armed Forces will naturally assist you in your mission: the success of the Cairo Accord is in all our interests, after all.'

I saw a snag. I saw several, not least of which was that I didn't want to go to Rome at all. I wanted to go back to dear old Blighty. I wanted to queue in a slow drizzle outside a chip shop in Islington. I wanted to watch the greyhounds race. These were not, however, things to mention to Major Fahd. Besides, I had a sudden worry. 'Has the hijacking received a lot of publicity?' I asked.

'I cannot tell you. It only occurred today. I have been in Djarouane on official business. I have heard nothing. Why?'

'Because the first question the British press always asks is whether there were any Britons aboard. I was travelling on a British passport, remember. There'll be a list of passengers in Athens, my name will be on it, and if I turn up in Rome some bright spark might well notice and want to ask a few questions, like who I am, how I escaped the hijack, and even why I was headed for Rome in the first place.'

'This is very true,' acknowledged Major Fahd. 'I must think.'

We had returned to the airport buildings by now, and got out of the Land Rover and into a more comfortable Range Rover driven by a man in uniform. The major sat in front, with me behind him. The vehicle with the pretty lady had already gone it seemed, and we soon followed, bumping along an inferior track that led through the dunes to the north. My eyes hurt – I needed some dark glasses – and the air-conditioning could only take the edge off the heat. 'Who built the airstrip?' I asked, conversationally. 'It seems a long way from anywhere.'

'It was built by the colonial French oppressors,' replied the major distractedly. Apparently he was still thinking. Then he turned on me and smiled. 'Unfortunately, it was not built to handle jumbo jets.' I think this was a joke.

Our vehicle bounced along the track, throwing up a heavy dust that marked where we had been. I felt like throwing up too, but whether it was the motion, or the shock of the hijack, I couldn't say. I looked at the major. For a long time there had been silence between us. Mind you, there wasn't really a lot to say: neither the weather nor the scenery offered much in the way of chit-chat, and apart from 'Do you come here often?' I couldn't think of a thing. Besides, I was hot, miserable and tired, and these were the least of my worries. But I didn't like the silence; I needed Major Fahd to like me. 'What are you thinking?' I asked.

'I am thinking there is only one solution,' said Major Fahd.

'Mmmmm?' I asked politely, while we bumped along the track.

'The meeting of the Cairo Accord signatories does not occur until late August,' said the major. 'You will have plenty of time.'

'Time for what?' I wondered.

'You are meant to be in Greece. Why, may I ask?'

'Holiday.'

'You say you are sending postcards daily from there?'

'Yes.'

'Despite this you are on a plane you were not on when it is hijacked?'

'That's one way of putting it.'

'Someone may spot the discrepancy?'

'I've already said all this.'

'I am recapitulating. In our business it is rare to have a full story: I am rather enjoying the novelty.'

'I'm glad to be of assistance.'

'I may continue then? Good. We must assume the worst. Someone will start asking questions about you, whatever you do. Therefore you will have to die.'

Oh – shit.

SEVEN

The major lit one of his French cigarettes. 'It shouldn't be too difficult to arrange,' he continued. 'You could have been either killed in the crash or shot by the hijackers; I'll leave the choice to you.'

Well, that is decent of you. My brain seemed incapable of making a decision and my mouth had to work on its own: there are those would say this was my normal state. 'The hijackers, please,' my mouth said.

'Good. I think, if you like, we could make it a hero's death. That would be suitable?'

'Just what I've always wanted,' confirmed my mouth.

'Excellent.' He took another pull at his cigarette and let the smoke escape. I fancied a cigarette, a last cigarette, to give some cinematic symmetry to my pointless mixed-up life and pointless mixed-up death. We topped a dune. Ahead, isolated, surprising in their greenery, were clumps of trees, and between the trees were buildings.

The major frowned. 'And now, we must make your travel arrangements.'

This was my death we were discussing: 'travel arrangements' seemed a dismissively weak euphemism. But this time when I had nothing to say I kept quiet, which just proves what a pickle I was in.

We approached the town. The tracks were better defined as they threaded through the trees and buildings; the buildings were low and tatty, overgrown white-washed breeze-blocks punched with window holes.

'Mmmm,' mused the major. 'We must decide on your journey. Overland would be best, I believe.'

Even my mouth had trouble responding to this, while my brain went completely AWOL. 'Overland?' I repeated. Perhaps he was talking about some desert equivalent of the River Styx.

'You still want to get to Rome, I take it,' the major said.

Ahead, reflecting the blue of the ridiculous sky, was a stretch of beautiful open water shaded by palms. The major saw my relief. 'Yes,' he said. 'It is good to be near water again. The desert can be an inhospitable place.'

The desert was as dry and dusty as a barrister's brief; the water looked clear and pure and gorgeous. But I was not thinking about that.

We drove on, past the oasis. The road was busier now, and metalled, though sprinkled with fine sand so our tyres made railway lines. According to the major it had been built, like the airstrip, by the French. At the roadside we saw the leggy coconut-matting remains of dead camels, and dented Citroens, abandoned and filling with sand, their shadows better defined than their bodywork. The sun, reddening like a boil, was sinking to our left. For a while the road went alongside a fat pipe, held above the desert on concrete pillars, then the pipe veered over the road in a welter of girders and valves and headed off, shimmering into nothing before it reached the horizon. Once a convoy of large trucks careered by, metal-ribbed and psychopathic, their lights fenced in by wire mesh. Later we passed a group of old men and older camels with legs crossed and toothy weatherbeaten grins. Then night fell, bang, like someone had switched off the lights, and we reached a town.

The major walked into the hotel with me and made the arrangements, barking out commands and receiving bows and submissions. I stood in the sparse lights of the foyer beneath a flyblown, overblown photograph of Qafadya's Patriotic Dictator, General Tassat, and looked around.

'We are now in Djarouane, capital of Saharan Qafadya,' said

Major Fahd. 'This is where you shall be staying until we can sort out the details of your journey.'

'Fine,' I said. Ahead, invitingly, was the doorway of a brighter room, where cigarette smoke wreathed beneath the light bulbs and tanned white men in bleached white suits lounged. The major followed my gaze. 'Yes, there are Europeans here, oilmen resting from the desert wells. But I do not advise contact. We have reason to believe that many of them are in the employment of foreign security agencies. You will be able to buy alcohol here, at least, which I imagine will suit your Irish tastes, but please drink it in your room. Here is your wallet.' I checked briefly through the credit cards. 'I hope you do not mind if I retain your passport: you will not be needing it again.'

My bag was taken from me by an elderly porter in a thick serge suit and I was led upstairs. 'I shall see you soon!' called the major. 'Have a pleasant stay.' From the lighted room came the unexpected, appropriate wail of The Platters' 'Smoke Gets In Your Eyes', an old favourite of mine, but I heeded the major's advice and climbed the reluctant stairs.

My room was small and the wall-to-wall uncarpeting, continued from the hall, combined artistically with the bleak white walls and the slumped bare mattress to give an atmosphere of consistent neglect. By the bed was a chest of drawers, faded and stained with the fuddled Olympic rings of long-finished drinks. There was a cheap and empty water jug on a prissy yellowing doily, and a copy of the Koran in the drawer like a Gideon's Bible. I sat on the mattress, by two folded sheets. A gecko, eight inches or so long, was splayed on the wall opposite me, beside the ubiquitous portrait of General Tassat, but when I stood it disappeared behind the frame. From downstairs I heard Elvis singing 'Separate Ways' on the jukebox. It had been my wife's dearest song, and heaven knows I'd loved it too. I was sad I could not go downstairs to listen, and sad for the past I had lost. The gecko reappeared on top of the picture frame, and eyed me reproachfully as if he knew my secret grief. I felt like chucking Gideon's Koran at him, but sat down on the bed instead. I am not normally given to compassion: were I sympathetic to others they might be sympathetic back, and what I have done mustn't be forgiven. Nor am I much given to introspection, for introspection sears me. But in that night and that respite, that remission from certain death, I did not harm my gecko. Instead I went to the door and called downstairs for a whisky, and while I waited, told the gecko my life story.

'I suppose you're asking yourself who I am,' I told him. 'Jack Diamond, they call me.' I corrected that. 'Jack Diamond, they called me, only now it seems Jack Diamond is dead, getting written out of the script as it were. So now I'm on my way to being nobody, with no past and not much of a future.' Again I corrected myself. 'That's not right,' I said. 'I've got a past. I've a past I'll never escape.' They were still playing 'Separate Ways' downstairs, and I got the feeling the gecko loved that tune too. This gave me a sense of comradeship and encouraged me to continue.

'So who am I, now that I'm not Jack Diamond?' I pondered, and fell into wordplay, my habitual way of pretending things are less desperate than they are. 'I guess I'm just a man, with private parts to play with and public parts to play.'

The gecko looked back at me. Normally at confessional you're wired in like the headlights of a desert truck, but here it was out in the open, and I could see from the gecko's eyes what he was thinking: 'All right, my son. Now let's get on with what you have to say.'

'You're quite right,' I admitted. But it was easier to make speeches than to make amends; I wanted to speak in a quiet monotone, to describe what had happened flatly, accurately, and instead produced an anguished howl. 'I haven't the words!' I realized. 'I can't say it . . . and it won't sound the same if I do!' If wordplay would not save me perhaps incoherence might.

But the gecko was not to be put off. 'There there, my son,' he said encouragingly. 'There there, there there, there there.'

I was as trapped in my Catholic habits as a monk but I controlled myself as best I could. There was a knock at the door. A barefooted lad in a fawn jerkin stepped in, handed me a glass of whisky from his tray, and left. I looked up at where the gecko was gummed to the wall, took a sip of the whisky, and continued. 'It was just after Christmas,' I told him. 'Michael, my son, was three. Santa had been: we'd had the Christmas turkey and the cold turkey and the turkey sandwiches and the turkey curry. I'd bought Michael . . .' A sob caught hold of my words: 'I'd bought him a fishing rod. His first rod. So we went up to the reservoir to fish. He sat next to me, close to me, imitating me, dangling his line in the water like he'd done this every Sunday afternoon of his life, like he was going to do it every Sunday afternoon from then on. I had my usual four-pack of Guinness with me, and there was a can of pop for him. Back home was his mother and sister, clearing the dinner, waiting, waiting like my own ma and sister had done when I was his age. It was cold and the fish wouldn't bite, but I didn't care. I was there with my boy and he was watching me, doing what I did, loving me as I was loving him.

'You know, he had this strange trick when he talked: he stuck "already" on the end of every sentence. I don't know where he picked that up. "This is good, isn't it, already?" he told me. And "Where are the fish, already?" when they wouldn't bite, like he was a little Jewish boy instead of Irish. And I loved him for it. He'd brought along a toy boat, another Christmas present, a little wooden yacht with real canvas sails, and because he was only three and because the fish wouldn't bite he was fooling about with it at the water's edge. And the bank was wet and slippery, and he fell in.

'I tried to wade in after him, but the bottom fell away steeply and I was splashing and swimming myself. I looked around for him, while the weight of my clothes dragged me down. I could see his boat just out of reach. I tried to dive for him but the clothes which a moment before had pulled me down were now full of air and holding me up. I tried to dive down and I couldn't.

'Someone else dived, a couple of young Prods, better swimmers than me. One of them helped me out, the other one found my Michael. They gave him the kiss of life, they did everything for him they could. But it was too late. The bloke handed him to me. There were tears in both our eyes. I held Michael in my arms. Michael, my son: he was everything to me and yet was nothing, nothing now, a yard of wet clothes and wide-open eyes. "Why didn't you save me, already?" those eyes said. And the worst of it was they still worshipped me, while in the centre of the dam his toy boat bobbed and mocked.

'I didn't stay long in Ireland after that. I didn't brave it out. I waited until the soil had covered his little coffin, I stayed long enough to hear the priest's comfortless comforting words, and then I was off, walking out on my family and my country because I could stand neither their reproach nor their sympathy. "Your son was too good for this world," the priest had said, and maybe so, but if I'd been someone else, if I had done something else, Michael would still be alive and my world would be the better for him. God knows it could not be worse.'

I wept a little, and then a little more. My gecko watched me, concerned and embarrassed. I think he'd have preferred it if I'd thrown the Koran.

I slept then, and it was morning. I was fully dressed on the bed, and the sun came through the window like a Panzer column. I felt strange and strangely rested: for the first night I could remember I had slept without bad dreams. Beside me on the chest of drawers was the glass of whisky, barely touched.

EIGHT

I went downstairs and ordered breakfast in incompetent French ('Petty dead journey, crass on aye cafay'). There were several oilmen there. They gave me the casual scrutiny of old lags; I said some polite 'good mornings', but made sure I sat well away.

Any interest they had in me was soon directed elsewhere. Major Fahd arrived, and with him the lovely lady from the plane. She wore a green camouflage outfit, with an open neck that displayed her interesting mole; her smock was tight at the waist and ankles, and loose everywhere else. She looked like a chic haversack. I looked at her and do believe I sighed.

'Mr Diamond,' said Fahd, shaking my hand in the nauseatingly eager American way: I bet he was a graduate of Harvard Business School. 'You had a good night's rest, I trust.'

Fine, I told him, eyeing the lady.

'Ah yes,' he continued. 'You have not been introduced. Major bar Hilai, of the Shin Beth; Mr Diamond of the INLA. Major bar Hilai has also been initiated into the, ahem, subject of our discussion of last night.' His speech was as soft as it was oblique: this was his country but our neighbours were not his countrymen.

'I am pleased to meet you,' said the lady major – the majorette.

'Delighted,' I said, in my best representative-of-the-Irish way. 'What's Shin Beth?'

'The Israeli internal security services.'

'Israeli!'

'Shhhh,' said the majors.

Major bar Hilai looked at me with contempt. It was one of *those* jokes – 'there was this Irishman, this Israeli and this Arab in the desert' – and even before the punchline I could see who would be the butt.

'Naturally the Israelis are involved in the, ahem, agreement signed in Egypt,' said Fahd in his curious urbane accent. 'They have, after all, one of the biggest stakes in the Middle East.'

Naturally . . .

Major bar Hilai was all charm. 'Major Fahd informs me that your security precautions were inadequate and that you are in all probability a wanted man. This was very careless of you; fortunately I think I am in a position to extricate you from your problem.'

'I wasn't exactly expecting to be hijacked,' I told her.

'Yours is an amateur organization, of course: such lack of foresight in a professional would be unforgivable.'

Like a road-mender hitting an ancient sewer she'd found a loyalty so long-buried I'd forgotten it was there. 'We may be amateurs but we haven't been entirely ineffective, you know,' I told her.

'Really? My knowledge of Northern European affairs is limited, but I was of the opinion that the high point of your activities was the bomb at the Droppin' Well discotheque in 1982. Eleven soldiers and six civilians died, I believe.'

'Major bar Hilai has a somewhat narrow view of terrorism,' said Major Fahd.

'I have a somewhat narrow view of murder,' said Major bar Hilai.

Maybe there was something noble and humane I should have said, but I was meant to be a senior officer in INLA so all I could manage was a weak 'War has its casualties.'

'A typically meaningless terrorist justification,' said Major bar Hilai, and I thought so too, but I needed their belief in me and would rather be detested than dead. 'What about the Israeli treatment of the Palestinians?' I countered. The shit – the ideology and intolerance I'd learned at my father's knee, my mother being more of a one for the Church – was really flowing from that ruptured sewer now.

'The Palestinians are terrorists too.'

'Their women and children?'

'And what of the innocent victims of terrorist attacks?' she answered.

This wasn't getting us anywhere; Major Fahd thought so too and coughed, signalling the end of Round One. 'Perhaps,' he said, 'we should concentrate on how you are to travel to Israel.'

'I don't want to go to Israel,' I reminded him.

'The arrangements have been made. You will travel through Israel, through the Lebanon and into Turkey. From Turkey you will go to Germany via Greece and Yugoslavia. From Germany a domestic European flight will take you to Rome.'

'You've organized all that since yesterday?' I couldn't have worked out a bus route in that time.

'We do not let the grass grow under our feet,' he said – a curious metaphor for a man who lived in the desert. 'And certain details remain to be finalized. But that is the plan in essence.'

'We shall have to travel to Israel together,' put in the majorette. She did not sound thrilled at the prospect. 'We cannot arrange two submarines at such short notice.'

'Submarines?' I rather fancied the idea.

'A technical term for illegal movements,' explained Fahd. 'You shall in fact be travelling by tramp ship.'

This sounded more my sort of transport, but I saw a snag. 'Isn't Qafadya entirely landlocked?'

'The word "entirely" in that sentence is redundant,' said bar Hilai – and what sort of bloody silly name is that anyway? '"Landlocked" alone would suffice.'

'The point is well-made, however,' put in Fahd diplomatically. 'We shall have to smuggle you into Algeria.'

'And I should appreciate it if you would leave the arrangements in our hands,' continued bar Hilai. 'I do not want any more bungling: if I had my way I would not help you at all, but Major Fahd seems to think it important.'

'For the sake of the, ahem, Egyptian agreement,' said Fahd.

'For the sake of the Accord,' she, less circumspect, agreed. 'However, you will please keep your suggestions to a minimum and your opinions to yourself.' She pulled back the elasticated wrist of her battle fatigues and looked at her watch. 'And now, Major Fahd, I think we have wasted enough time here. We have other people to see.' She didn't actually say that the others were more important, but then she didn't have to. They left, and I finished my cup of cold *café au lait*.

There didn't seem to be much for me to do. I wandered back to my room for another chat with the gecko but he wasn't around: maybe he'd heard me coming. So I lay on the bed until the room got too hot, then decided to look round the town.

The hotel was on a fair-sized square. In the middle was a group of sorry-looking plane trees, their trunks spotty and tall as giraffes' necks and their leaves dried like bay leaves; to the left was La Banque Qafadya (a sort of fake Versailles pavilion faded to off-white), and to the right a building marked, in depleted stencilled lettering, L'HOTEL, which probably meant it was the town hall. It looked shabbier than the place I was staying in, so I didn't investigate. There weren't many people about: a couple of vase-shaped veiled ladies walked by, and a negro with a sub-machine gun stood in front of the town hall chewing the butt of a damp cigar. I walked left, past the bank, and down a side street.

Here I saw more people, though no more activity. Groups of men sat in doorways or under striped canopies, occasionally gobbing into brass spitoons. Each man's crumpled face looked like an unsavoury rose: the outer petals were the cloth folds of their headgear; the inner petals were dewlaps and wrinkles of desiccated flesh; in the centre was a ring of shorn grey beard and a handful of ugly yellow-stained teeth. The men squinted at me as I passed, but without curiosity.

I reached a larger street, where wider canopies shaded shady second-hand saddles. There were snakes in woven baskets there, and bowls of unappetizing fly-covered figs. There were children there too, and noises. Shopkeepers called out their wares and shoppers haggled grimly; goats bleated and transistors blared; motor-scooters revved and roared, rearranging the dust. The children began to follow me and demand baksheesh, but I didn't think they'd take my credit cards and pressed on. The children didn't seem to care – perhaps they did take my cards – and followed me anyway. So did the flies.

The road was paved with stone, uneven but enduring, and between the stones were puddles of fine white dust. I carried on along the street. The heat still hurt, the flies still swarmed, and I felt like the Pied Piper with those kids still following me – there was even a little lame boy at the back who couldn't keep up. The street wound and split between the low white breeze-block houses. The road climbed a hill and then dropped. There was a garage with old-fashioned pumps, where a couple of battered jeeps were being cannibalized for spare parts. The petrol gave the air an extra shimmer, and I saw a snake slide between the stones at the foot of a well; I passed a couple more wells, a hundred crude wooden ladders, and a dozen or so camels; then, keeping up the theme of snakes and ladders, I found myself back at the square where I'd started. The hotel bar was open and empty so I had a warm beer and then another. I wandered over to the jukebox. The selections were all in English but the coins it took were Qafadyan, and the titles only fanned my nostalgia. But it wasn't a bad nostalgia, and my past seemed more a cause for sorrow than despair. I had a third beer and realized my thirst was due to the heat and not my past. With that realization came another, even more unfamiliar. I realized I was happy.

Another European came into the bar behind me, with a newspaper under his arm. He ordered a whisky on the rocks. I looked up at him incuriously, and then spluttered the beer back in my glass. It was the bloke with the harelip. He hadn't even changed his suit, but neither had I.

For a moment I thought he was going to pretend he hadn't seen me, but then he must have decided that would be silly, and with pretended calm he unfolded his paper. I could pretend calm as well as him, and turned back to the bar to finish my beer.

He had joined me by the time I put the glass down. 'Having another one?' he asked, rather nervously.

'Thanks.'

'Perhaps you'd get one for me, would you?' He smiled, as if expecting rejection. 'Only the cheque I'm expecting hasn't arrived yet.'

His drink arrived, and we were silent a while, like lovers on a first date. Then we both spoke at once. 'What brings you to . . . Sorry . . . No, you first.'

'Business,' he said. 'A little business.' He drank his beer off and ordered another. I had the feeling I'd be paying. 'Let's sit down,' he said, with a meaningfully suspicious, I-bet-that-man's-paid-to-listen look at the barman.

We went to his table, where the folded newspaper still lay. 'Call me Chambers,' he said, which isn't quite the same as 'My name's Chambers.'

'I'm Jack Diamond,' I told him, as we shook hands and sat.

'I know,' he said. 'I was following you in Salonika, remember. Not my usual job, tagging people. But they were short-staffed. You work for Flaherty.'

I drank some beer and said nothing. Chambers still looked like the remittance man in a 1950s adaptation of a Somerset Maugham story, but that might just be his cover.

'Fancy us meeting here,' he said, like he meant it. 'I'm in Djouarane on a little job.' He leaned close, and I smelled his breath. He'd been eating goat's bottom. 'Have you still got the book?' he asked.

'What book?'

He managed to look crafty and disappointed at the same time, which isn't easy unless you have a naturally shifty face.

'All right,' I said. 'I'll tell you about the book if you'll tell me about the Cairo Accord.'

At this a crack appeared in the white bristles of his stubble, so

I thought he was smiling. 'The Cairo Accord,' he repeated.

It was my turn to look disappointed, but he was used to disappointing people and still did not speak.

'Come on,' I said. 'Information for information.'

'You're asking about the wrong information,' he protested, like I wasn't playing the game right.

'Well, what do you want to tell me?' I asked.

'Don't you want to know who I work for?'

'I suppose I do.'

He nodded. 'Bet you think it's MI5 or MI6, don't you?'

I hadn't really thought about it, to be honest, but as he was British, party to dangerous secrets, yet too tatty to be a VAT man, MI6 seemed a likely employer. I shrugged. 'Okay.'

'You're wrong.'

Nothing new in that.

'Aren't you going to ask me then?' Chambers continued.

'All right: who do you work for?'

'MI7,' he said promptly.

'Who the sweet baby Jesus is that?'

'It's like MI5 and MI6, only more important. Look.' He handed me a card. It had his photograph, and a Ministry of Defence stamp, and under department 'MI7' was inked in. It actually looked rather genuine, though the name had been crudely whited out.

'What does 'MI7' do then?'

He drew me by the elbow until I was even closer, and looked carefully to either side before speaking. 'You don't imagine the antics of MI5 and MI6 to be the limits of British intelligence do you? That's just window-dressing, display for public consumption. My department operates behind the scenes.'

'How come I've never heard of you?'

'We're a secret organization,' he said. Now why didn't I think of that? 'And anyway, we're not so much spies as civil servants, and we operate in line with normal civil service procedure.'

'What does that mean?'

'It means we keep quiet about all our activities except the

71

cock-ups, and then we keep very quiet.' He seemed happy enough to talk though. 'We started in the Second World War, but got important afterwards. All the Allied powers built up first-rate intelligence networks in Germany, and after the war it looked as if they would be wasted. We hit on a scheme, though, and gave the Russians West Germany for their spies to play in while we kept the East. A perfect solution.'

'Very ingenious,' I admitted, when I'd worked it out. 'But why are you telling me this? You're part of British intelligence. You know who I am: I'm a courier for the INLA. I'm the last person you should be talking to!'

'But you're going to tell me about the book?' He was wheedling. 'Aren't you?'

I hate to see a grown man wheedle. 'Well,' I started. 'On the outside it says *Advanced Mathematical Tables*, but that's just a cover.' I was pleased with the pun; he missed it. 'And on the inside . . . Behind you! Get down quick!'

He ducked; I sprinted from the room like the Hounds of Hell were behind me. Chambers's story about MI7 was probably bullshit, but it was better-quality bullshit than any I could produce about *Advanced Mathematical Tables*.

NINE

I wandered around Djouarane again, then returned to the hotel, checking the bar carefully on my way in. The Englishman didn't seem to be there, but that didn't mean he wouldn't be coming round later. I swallowed a quick snort of scotch and went to my room. I didn't know if he was a British agent or a lying bore, but either way I was happier avoiding him. Besides, I was knackered.

Hurricane had left a loose red over the middle bag. I cued easily and dropped it, rolling up the table with a good angle for the black, but just as I was taking aim some bloody fool spoke my name and I found myself blinking my way into unexpected darkness. Either the lights had failed during my World Championship eliminator at the Crucible or I was waking up in a crummy hotel in the Sahara with a gun barrel pressing the gap between my jawbone and my ear.

'Wake up, Mr Diamond,' the voice repeated, softly. It was a woman's voice. 'And please lie still.' There was a delicate fragrance of perfume in the air, a scent like innocence betrayed.

I still had the rosary bead click of snooker balls in my ears but I knew the accent. 'Major bar Hilai?'

'Do as I ask and you will not be hurt.'

It was nice to be given a choice. I seemed to have fallen asleep on my bed fully dressed, for the second night in a row. Whatever had become of hygiene? I remember High Jean, she was an air hostess. But this seemed no time for reminiscence. 'What do you want?' I asked.

'Information.'

Well, she had certainly come to the right place: I was so

73

well-informed I could make the lead story in a tabloid read like the Encyclopaedia Britannica. 'Such as?'

'We will begin with your mission. Why were you on the Athens-Rome flight?'

There was no point in lying. 'I was to deliver a book to an address in Rome.'

'What was the address?'

'I'm not sure.' The barrel of the gun pushed harder into my head and the pressure must have stimulated my brain. 'Ria Mazzanati. 287.'

She nodded as if she had expected as much. 'And what was in the book?'

Here we go again! 'I don't know. Just a lot of numbers. Major Fahd's got it now.'

The gun barrel moved down my face and was cold as the desert night against my cheek. 'Please do not mess with me, Mr Diamond.'

'I'm not messing!'

'Shhh. The hotel has many listening devices. I do not think Qafadyan Intelligence has reason to be tuned to you, but if they make a random sweep through the frequencies they may take note if they hear us speak; whispering they will not pick up, unless they are specifically listening for it, because it blurs with the noises of retuning.'

'I'm not messing!' I repeated, as emphatically as I could in a whisper, and I must have been getting better at emphatic whispers because she let me carry on. 'I'm just the messenger boy. Honest. You said yourself I was a bloody fool; do I act like I know what's going on?'

'Just tell me your story.'

So I did, starting with how I'd been involved with the INLA way back, going through briefly to the night Flaherty had called, and explaining how Mulligan had dropped word of the Cairo Accord. She stopped me there: 'And this was the first time you had heard of the Accord?'

'That's right.'

'Continue with your tale,' she said, and I knew she believed me by the way the gun slumped on to the pillow away from my head. I described how I'd floored the policeman, stayed in the safe house, and flown to Thessalonika. She'd been hijacked as well of course, so there wasn't much to tell from there, though she showed interest in Mr Chambers from MI7. 'And that's it,' I concluded.

The cow was laughing. 'What's so funny?' I asked her.

'Oh, Mr Diamond, your poor Mr Flaherty. Rogue agents occur frequently, of course, but they generally sabotage the operation deliberately. Yet your sabotage has been particularly effective, and entirely accidental.'

'It's not exactly my fault things haven't worked out.'

'No.' She was still chuckling. 'Not your fault, though perhaps to hit the policeman was a little extreme, and I think Mr Flaherty must be very worried about you.'

'Tough on Mr Flaherty,' I said. 'I never wanted to be involved.'

'Of course, you were never the genuine courier, but what your Mr Flaherty obviously intended as a cheap diversion must be now costing him a great deal in anxiety.'

'Diversion?'

'Obviously you are a decoy. However short of agents he was, your Mr Flaherty was unlikely to trust this mission to an amateur, after all.'

'So there's nothing in the book worth knowing?'

'Probably not.' Her perfume caressed the air. 'Would *you* trust anyone as incompetent, inexperienced and incapable as you?'

'Possibly not,' I said. 'But thanks a bundle for the character reference.'

'I am sorry, Mr Diamond,' she said, but she was not apologizing for the insults to my pride. 'You are not the man I thought. I came here tonight to interrogate you on the Cairo Accord; I thought you might be able to add a few details, help me fill in the picture.' She laughed quietly, easily, and I saw her teeth in the dark. 'Do you know, if the threat of violence hadn't worked, I was prepared to seduce you to find out what I wanted? Can you imagine!'

I could.

'However,' she continued, while my prick, more optimistic than the rest of me, flexed its muscles in my trousers, 'there is fortunately no longer the need for such measures; I will leave you to sleep, and of course, I shall not say a word to Major Fahd.' Her disembodied teeth grinned at me. 'Pleasant dreams.'

My frustration was not only sexual. 'Hang on,' I said. 'Perhaps you could tell me a few things?'

'Such as?'

'What's the Cairo Accord? What's an Israeli intelligence agent doing consorting with Qafadyan intelligence? And what's going to happen to me now you know I'm a nobody?'

She thought for a little while. 'I can see why these things might interest you,' she said. 'On the other hand I am not sure how far I can go in explaining them to you. I was not briefed to handle this situation; officially I should not answer your questions at all.'

'And unofficially?' I gave her my most charming smile, but it was dark so this didn't put her off.

'The Cairo Accord works on two levels at least,' she said. 'On the one hand it is a way that terrorist organizations can pool resources, exchange practical information and group together to gain greater economic weight; on the other hand it is a means by which various security and intelligence agencies can monitor the activities of the terrorists.'

'Don't the terrorists mind?'

'I do not think they are aware of the extent of our penetration; they permit a certain degree of co-operation, of course, as an economy measure. Co-operation within a competitive environment is often cheaper than competition, and of course the Cairo Accord is essentially an economic rather than an ideological grouping. Ideologically, few of the signatory organizations could agree on whether the sun rises in the west or east; economically speaking, however, their aims are broadly similar.'

'So it's all about money, in other words.'

'My dear Mr Diamond,' she said, and a little sexual thrill went through me, replaced almost at once by a sense of mounting confusion. 'Of course it is all about money. Economics underpins our age as religion did in earlier times. Europe used to be divided on religious lines – Protestant versus Catholic. Men are always encouraged to fight when they are fighting for something they believe in deeply, and today they believe in economics. The fundamental difference between East and West is a simple matter of economic theory, communism versus capitalism, and both sides are prepared to spend more than they have, in order to prove the superiority of their own system. Indeed, it is the fact that both sides *are* spending more than they have that makes an agreement such as the Accord necessary.

'All the organizations involved in the Accord have two things in common. One is that they operate outside the normal regulations; the other is that they require money. These factors apply as much to security organizations as to terrorist organizations, and therefore both types require clandestine funding. Think of the problems President Reagan had getting funds to the Contras. The Cairo Accord is a way of laundering money, and that money, the product of illegal arms sales, bank robberies, kidnappings, extortion or whatever, is what keeps the Accord going.'

I sat up on the bed. 'All right. But earlier today you were laying into me because you thought I was a terrorist . . .'

'I have apologized.' The warmth suddenly left her voice: she was anticipating criticism, and she was right.

'Apology accepted. But there you were, beating seven bells out of me, and here you are now, calm as you like, talking about kidnapping and extortion and God knows what else. Where's your morality now?'

'I was *describing* the Cairo Accord. I do not approve of it. I do not approve of leprosy but I have to accept that it exists. And now I must leave you. I believe I have answered all your questions.'

'You've missed out the most important one: what's going to happen to me.'

'I don't know. But I will say nothing to jeopardize your position.

Good night.' Her voice was cool but human, and I wanted to keep her in the room.

'One last thing. Why have you explained the Accord to me like this?'

'You may need the information to bluff your way past Major Fahd.'

'But what if I tell someone about it, or about you letting me in on the secret?'

'Mr Diamond, I do not think you will have the opportunity. Do you? And now, I really must bid you goodnight.' The door opened, her graceful body slipped out and I was alone where her perfume lingered.

A day or two passed. I looked out for Major bar Hilai but didn't see her; I looked out for the Englishman too, so I could duck if he was coming, but he wasn't around either. The only person I saw was Major Fahd, who brought news that we'd be leaving Qafadya in a day or so, and a copy of the *Daily Telegraph*. My death was announced on page three, column one. Major Fahd had promised me a hero's death. According to the *Daily Telegraph*, at least, I had died as I had lived, as a statistic. But it was the first time I'd ever made the national press, and I was chuffed about that.

In fact, come to think of it, I was chuffed by any number of things. I was relieved by Major bar Hilai's notion there was nothing important in *Advanced Mathematical Tables*. This meant I didn't need to feel guilty about cocking up Flaherty's mission: I still had a ghost of a loyalty to Republicanism. And it meant I didn't need to feel guilty about being involved in the first place, because I wasn't carrying the formula for a nuclear bomb or a nerve gas after all. So there was a double cause for celebration.

I also felt better for my chat with the gecko. Talking has got me into a lot of trouble over the years, but just once in a while it helps.

And then there was the fact that I was alive, which, now I thought about the hijack, seemed pretty miraculous in itself. I hadn't been killed by the terrorists, I'd survived the crash-landing, Major Fahd hadn't put a bullet through my brain, and Major bar

Hilai hadn't given me away. And finally, perversely, came the fact that I was officially dead, which relieved me and released me, though I could not at the time have said just why.

All in all then, it was a pretty cheerful me who, one desert night, stood on an outcrop of sand-dusted stone above Djouarane and counted the stars. Below me there was an abandoned fort that came straight from *Beau Geste*, and a stubby minaret above the gold dome of a mosque. Higgledy-piggledy rows of two-storey houses danced by the light of the moon, and along the valley, in each direction, I saw desert. The white town on the white sand looked like Bethlehem; I felt peace and tranquillity and simplicity, and of course it didn't last.

TEN

KERKRASH!! It didn't. The planes came from the north, loaded with bombs and marked with the stars and bars of the United States. KAPOW!! They dragged their roar behind them like a trawl-net, and the first bombs were exploding by the time the noise of the jets arrived. KERRUMP!! Then everything became noise, everything but the orange flashes with white centres that split open the desert night. KARRANG!! Djouarane had no defence. KERRAH!! I stood on the dune and watched the town burn. Fizzing uneven lines of white fire erupted from the explosions, staying on the retina long after they'd left the air. KERWHAM!! The planes were sleek rapists. KAZZAM!! I saw bouquets of flame and wreaths of smoke. KA-THUMP!! While the trawl-net of sound was uprooting the town there was no way of hearing the shrieks, but as the planes faded to a distant drone and then nothing, their noise was replaced by wild screams. I heard shock and pain and grief, bewilderment and fury, and the sound of falling buildings. Homes turned into crematoria.

KAZZAM-KAZZING-KAZOOM!!

After the bombardment I went back to the hotel. The bombs had mostly fallen on the far side of the town, missing the public buildings and falling square on the casbah. I did not pass much damage, just anguish and incomprehension. The flames were mounting high above the casbah, and the streets were full of running figures. I stood aside to let them pass. They wore dark robes and as they ran they put their hands to their tipped-back faces, raised their elbows high and wailed for their dead.

I hoped to God no one would take me for an American.

Most of the guests were in the foyer of the hotel. They looked scared. I looked for Chambers, the Englishman. He was standing by the door of the bar. He still wore the same suit but at least he'd had a shave. Maybe his cheque had come through. I was not sure I wanted to speak to him but at least he was a familiar face in the senselessness of death that was all around us. He saw me too, and smiled a smile that was like a slice of lemon in the bottom of an empty glass. He started to approach, but then a lovely woman with a mole on her neck strode into the hotel with a machine pistol at her hip. Several guests screamed but Major bar Hilai ignored them and ushered me out into the street. A Land Rover stood waiting.

'Very dramatic,' I told her. 'What about my luggage?'

'Shut up,' she said, hurrying me into the back of the truck. 'We are in a great hurry. Just do as you are told.' I wasn't sure how things stood between us, but I hoped she was only being curt because Major Fahd was sitting in the front. I sat down and the Land Rover accelerated through the ravished town. Poor Bethlehem. Behind us, Chambers came out in the street and watched us leave, just as he had done in Thessalonika. It was a pose that seemed to suit him.

'We have decided to set off for Algeria tonight,' said Major Fahd. 'This imperialist American terrorism means Major bar Hilai will not be safe in Qafadya. Israel is too good a friend to America, Major.'

His phrase about imperialist American terrorism sounded like so much well-rehearsed bullshit, but his face was tight and his voice was full of anger. Qafadya was his country after all, and these were his countrymen dying.

'What's the plan?' I asked.

'You shall travel with Major bar Hilai, as arranged, but your route has been modified. Now, take off your clothes please, both of you, and change into the burnouses you will find in the back of this vehicle.'

I looked at Major bar Hilai, who smiled back at me in an amused fashion and began, with tantalizing slowness, to unfasten the buttons of her combat gear. 'Take off all your clothes,' repeated Fahd. 'If you are arrested or shot I want you to be anonymous Arabs; anonymous Arabs do not shop at Marks and Spencer.'

Neither do I. Meanwhile, still looking at me in her amused, provocative way, Major bar Hilai slipped first one shoulder and then the other out of her fatigues, wriggled, and let them fall to the floor. She was wearing only underpants, and not much of them; her breasts were full and pale, and her nipples stood proudly and stared into my eyes while the light of the burning town moved around her and over her and into her. My prick stretched towards her as though greeting an old friend.

'What are you waiting for, Mr Diamond?' she asked. 'You must get changed too.'

I didn't fancy her seeing me with a prick as long, hard and tricky to handle as a punt pole. I tried to ignore the fact that she was lowering her pants – revealing luxuriant curled black hair in a lush triangle, and then turning round lusciously, bending down with shapely legs and curved buttocks that flexed beneath smooth soft flesh as she sorted out her new costume – and I failed, so I had to turn my back when peeling off my Y-fronts and hope she'd put the odd-shaped shadows down to the effect of the light from the fires. Out of the corner of my eye I saw that Major Fahd was watching her intently. I cannot say I blamed him.

The burnous is a curious garment, a sort of nappy-and-cloak combination, and I was finding it almost impossible to sort out. Major bar Hilai leaned across the limited space in the back of the Land Rover and tugged me into shape. She was fully dressed now – no one is more fully dressed than a person in a burnous – and I'd at least sorted out the nappy bit, so modesty and propriety were restored, though her naked body remained on my retina like the after-image of the fires.

I took my wallet from my trousers, but as I was searching for somewhere to conceal it Major Fahd spoke: 'Please take nothing that could in any way identify you as a European,' he said, so I put my wallet back into my trousers. This bothered me a bit. If I was going to die – literally or not – I might as well die beyond my means.

'Can I take my pistol?' asked Major bar Hilai.

'What make is it?'

'Uzi.'

'Very well. They are not unknown among the border tribes.'

While they were talking I surreptitiously took out my credit cards and tucked them into the crotch of my burnous. I had the feeling I might need them yet.

We were leaving the town by now, speeding along one of the French highways and going west, towards Algeria. The red glow of Djouarane was soon lost in the desert night.

It was a monotonous journey. Only one incident of note occurred all night: Major bar Hilai asked me to call her Rebecca so I asked her to call me Jack. Major Fahd noticed this new familiarity and remarked on it. 'We have a long journey ahead of us,' said Rebecca. 'I shall suspend my hostility to Jack Diamond and terrorism until we reach Israel.'

Major Fahd nodded. 'Very professional,' he acknowledged.

We started to travel again when the sun rose. 'It would have been better to travel by night,' said Fahd, 'but in the rush to get you out of Djouarane we were unable to make the full preparations. I dare not be out of Djouarane for long; I hope you do not mind.'

As usual I didn't seem to have a lot of choice. By midday the June sun was incredible, making an elongated mirage of the road surface that looked like an almost vertical ribbon of water. We didn't have enough spit to talk, and anyway had nothing to say, so we travelled mostly in silence. After three-quarters of a day's travel, and frequent stops to refuel from cans piled in bunkers along the way, we saw mountains ahead. The mountains were queer lumps of rock that rose almost sheer from the desert. 'El-Hoggar,' said Major Fahd. He said it grimly, but even 'Happy Birthday' would have sounded grim in that heat.

We were a long time reaching the mountains but at last we were there, and the road began to thrash, epileptically, between the rockfaces. We climbed high, the road swinging out over gut-guttering drops and then burrowing between narrow cliffs, until we reached a roadside shrine, and there we stopped. 'The Algerian border is forty miles away,' said Major Fahd. 'But I, sadly, must leave you here.'

Rebecca and I climbed down. The cross had been removed from the shrine, leaving it as desolate as an empty birdcage. I sat by it with my legs splayed. It really was bloody hot. 'How long are we going to have to wait?' I asked, squinting up at him.

'Not long, I hope,' he replied. 'Your guide should be here within the hour.' He fetched a large bag, the sort I'd seen before on ageing hippies – two bits of rug sewn together with a fringe at the bottom and a shoulder strap on top. 'You will need this,' he told me.

I took it from him. It was heavy.

'And now I must get back to Djouarane.' His impeccable white suit looked thoroughly pecked by now, and his dark hair was grey with dust, but he was still a handsome man. 'I wish you the best of luck,' he said, and I think he meant it.

He climbed back into the Land Rover and waved. His driver reversed it and turned round. We watched him drive away.

'Hot,' remarked Rebecca, when he had gone.

'Very,' I replied.

If this was to be the limit of conversation we were in for a dull time. Fahd had left us a water bottle, and the fringed bag, and Rebecca had her gun. A game of I-Spy might have been appropriate but it certainly wouldn't have taken long. Besides, it was really hot now. Djouarane had been quite hot enough, thanks, but there the edge of the heat had been blunted by the buildings; here everything was raw.

The sun shifted through the mountains, and the shadows lengthened, but the rocks were still hot. 'Time for a drink,' said Rebecca bar Hilai, and I agreed.

'What's in the bag?' she asked.

'I don't know.' I felt in it. 'That's useful,' I told her.

'What is it?'

'*Advanced Mathematical Tables*. What else could it be?'

She smiled in consolation. It was a good smile and I was consoled. She handed me the water.

'Have you spent much time in the desert?' I asked after I'd drunk.

'Only when I was very young.' The drink made talking possible again. 'I was born a kibbutzim, but my father was unhappy there. I was brought up in Tel Aviv.'

'How did you become a spy?'

'I am not a spy,' she said severely. 'I am involved in counter-espionage.'

The distinction seemed slight but I wasn't going to argue. 'All right. How did you get involved in counter-espionage?'

'Because I am good at it. I am a Jew, Mr Diamond . . . '

'Jack,' I reminded her.

'I am a Jew. My country is hard-pressed. It is the duty of all Israelis to serve our country in whatever way we can.'

'Fair enough. I'm an Irishman,' I said. 'I was brought up to believe the same.'

'There is a note of scepticism in your voice,' she prompted.

I agreed. 'I don't believe it any more. Not all of it anyway. I mean, I believe that all Ireland should be a Republic, of course, and I believe that it will be some day. But I no longer believe in murder.' I smiled, and the skin of my lips cracked. 'But we've had this conversation before. Only that time it was you saying my lines. I know which story I believe; how about you?'

She looked past me, past the wayside shrine and the narrow dirt road, to the jagged crags where the mountains cut into the sky. 'Don't press me, Jack Diamond,' she said. Her voice was quiet. 'I know there's truth in what you say. But don't press me. I've invested too much of myself in Israel. I've even invested my pride.'

So I didn't press. I didn't know what she was talking about, then, but I didn't press.

It was too hot. We grew weaker and more tired, and neither of us said anything. To begin with, we stayed silent because we did not want to talk about terrorism; later, because we did not want to talk of death. Our death. For the day was wearing on and we were wearing out, and in the oven-heat of the mountains our strength was ebbing fast. I would not have believed we could weaken so quickly. If the guide did not arrive soon he would be too late.

I had only recently died the first time.

I really didn't want to die again.

ELEVEN

Night fell, and so did we, sleeping close together against the chill. Neither of us slept well. Rebecca clutched the water bottle close to her all night, as if she feared I would steal it. Which I guess I might have done, given the chance.

I woke from a fevered dream to find that the sun had come back. Nothing had changed, nor was it going to change: as the day grew longer so did the shadows, but the heat remained the same. We sat in the middle of the bleakest landscape on God's earth. No: correct that. This wasn't God's earth. God's earth is green and fertile; it has trees and rivers and gambolling lambs, and above it go fluffy white clouds. This was someone else's earth, some other deity, the same one who'd laid waste to the moon.

Rebecca offered me the water bottle. 'Only a mouthful,' she said.

I nodded. 'Where exactly are we?' I asked. I wanted to make sure we weren't on the moon.

'I'm not certain,' said Rebecca. 'Near the Algerian border?'

There was a third reason now for not talking. We'd run out of spit. But I tried anyway. 'This is the Hoggar range,' I said.

'That's right.' And as before, she looked beyond me, through me, towards the mountains and the sky. The conversation was over.

These were not mountains as I understood the term. Mountains are pointed and have snow on the top. They look like wise old men. The Hoggar mountains were blunt and bald, as ugly as spoilheaps and just as desolate. Tufts of wiry bleached grass came through cracks in the rock. A flat wind shifted the grit. Nothing else happened. 'Is there nothing we can do?'

'There is nothing to be done,' she replied.

We sounded like a couple of characters from *Waiting for the Toilet*, but she was right of course. There was nothing to be done. 'Can't we carry on walking,' I said, the words already getting burdensome in my desiccated mouth.

'Which way?'

'Not the way we came.' A pause for breath and to drag up some spittle for the next phrase. 'There's nothing there.'

'True.'

'The other way then. Yes?'

'Our guide should meet us here,' she said, then shrugged and got to her feet. 'But I don't suppose he'll miss us if we stay on the road.'

Walking had seemed like a good idea. But it wasn't. For a lot of reasons. We were being drained of all lubrication and were seizing up like old cars. Our brains were evaporating. We had no shoes. We would never even get as far as the eye could see, never mind to anywhere worth seeing. And we were dying.

The long journey in the Land Rover had taken its toll, and this walk in the heat was finishing us off. The heat was everywhere, bouncing round the rocks and tugging at my burnous. We had another drink – it soaked into the dried-out cells of my tongue – then walked a little more. Walked. Limped. Staggered. And fell.

I went first, but only by seconds. It was as if the only thing that had kept her going was that I was walking too, because she collapsed next to me, gratefully, diving on to the soil. I tried to say something to her. Nothing happened. No noise came out and she did not move.

We had travelled less than a mile.

I think I slept then, and my dreams were even more fevered than before. Another night must have come, because when I woke I was being shaken and I could not see a thing.

My eyes adjusted after a moment, and I could make out who my new companion was. He wore a black cowl and a black veil. He was Death.

As I blinked in my sleepiness and fear he addressed me. He spoke in a garble of curious noises, a spitting language in a world without spit, a nimble tongue in a land where tongues are swollen and black, a death rattle. 'I – can't – understand,' I said.

The night was not quite as dark as Death's clothes. I could see the white of one eye as he peered at me closely. There were lines threaded through to the pupil, and the pupil was black like a void. The other eye seemed entirely absent. I wondered if Death was a Cyclops. It was a notion that made as much sense as any other at that time.

The eye squinted at me. 'Yeengleesh?' he asked.

'I – I'm – I'm – Irish,' I said, weakly.

'Yeenglish,' he said, as though I'd confirmed something. 'Hi.'

I don't know much about Death, but I know Death doesn't say 'Hi'.

'You like a sommating to dink?'

I nodded, dumbly. As my eyes adjusted further I saw him better, but could still see only one eye, and no mouth.

He lifted a leather bottle from his belt and held it to my lips. The water smelled of goat, leather and urine, and come to think of it so did he. 'Thanks,' I said when I'd drunk, and my speech now sounded like words.

'I Imrad. You call?'

'Diamond. Jack Diamond.'

'Jacques?' He said it in the French way.

'Oui,' I said, to be helpful, but Imrad shook his head.

'Not spik French,' he said, and spat. 'French, spbahch.'

'Sure,' I said. The English feel that way about the French too. The Irish feel that way about the English.

He pointed at himself. 'Amazigh.'

'Amazigh?' How many names did he have?

'Targui.'

I learned later what Amazagh and Targui meant: Amazagh is the singular of Imazighen, which is what the Tuareg tribesmen call themselves, and Targui is the singular of Tuareg, which is what the Arabs call them. As it happens Imrad isn't a name either, it's a Tuareg rank. But I never did learn his name, so 'Imrad' will have to do.

He left me to revive Rebecca. She was as far gone as me, and clutched the air weakly, scratching away imaginary demons. Then Imrad lit a fire, and I could see him properly. I could also see Rebecca, and she wasn't a pretty sight: her lips were cracked and blistered, and her nose and forehead had sloughed their skin in wide transparent bands like drying glue. I don't suppose I looked any better. It was morning before we had revived enough to be really sure of what was happening – we both lapsed back into unconsciousness and I guess what we really needed was hospitalization. Imrad was equipped for the desert, designed for it, dressed head to foot in what looked like black but was actually dark blue, except for a sort of white underskirt, and one of his eyes was hidden behind a patch. A scar started above and finished below the patch. It was difficult to gauge his age from what little was exposed: he was either a healthy septuagenarian or a thirty-year-old who'd had problems.

The fire died as the sun came up. Rebecca said something in Arabic to Imrad, and he replied in the same language.

'Hey,' I said. 'Cut that out. Imrad here speaks English.'

'Sure,' he agreed. 'Speek Yeengleesh, no French, Spinach, Arhahbique.'

'Spinach?' I asked, catching Rebecca's eye.

'Most certainly excellent Spinach.'

'I was asking how he found us,' said Rebecca to me. She turned back to Imrad. 'Did Major Fahd tell you to look for us?'

'Fahd, pspattt!' he said, which could have meant anything and probably meant yes.

'Thank you very much,' I said – polite if not quite appropriate. Though Christ knows he had earned our thanks.

'Is OK. You feeling better now.'

'Much better.' I was feeling awful, but he was right: it was an improvement on how I'd felt before.

Imrad's one eye looked at me solicitously. 'Now you drinked water you want drink. Whisky-vodka-redrum?'

'What have you got there?' I asked. 'A cocktail cabinet?'

'Not cocktail, camel tail,' Imrad replied. He laughed. He liked to laugh at his own jokes.

He handed me what looked like a wine bottle without a label; I couldn't say what was in it. Probably the whisky-vodka-redrum and a healthy splash of whatever NASA used to put a man on the moon.

'I didn't think Arabs drank alcohol,' I said, when I'd finished gagging.

'Not Arab,' he told me sternly. 'Me Berber, Imazighen. Arabs stink!' Imrad stank too, like a heavy-duty armpit, so this was a real case of the pot calling the kettle an illegal substance. 'Fuck Arabs!'

'You speak good English,' I lied, to be friendly. 'Where did you learn it?'

'General Patton he at my village. Maybe I was three, father dead, missing, gone, mother alone with me. Some GI fucker sleep with her, teach me American, huckleberry pie, home run, bubblegum card, nylons. Later I fix him, knife here,' – he thumped his own left kidney with a clenched hand – 'leave him for vultures. Now, sometimes Imrad works for dope runners, Morocco-Spain, they speak English. Where you learn speak English?'

'Just picked it up as I went along, I guess, like you.'

'C'est langue très facile, buono, buono,' said Imrad or the drink. Perhaps he spoke all languages equally badly, was multilingually incoherent. It was an odd thought. 'How you doing, fucker?' he asked me. He reached across, took over the drink and had another swig. 'You good pisser?'

I wasn't sure whether this was a literal question, but there was nothing in me to piss anyway. 'So-so.'

'I good pisser. Piss over camel.'

'Doesn't the camel mind?'

'I piss over top. You piss over top?'

'I've never tried it.'

Rebecca, less at ease in a drunken conversation in the desert dawn than I, was clutching her gun through the folds of her burnous. 'I think it's time we moved on,' she said.

Imrad stood and shrugged. 'She like my woman,' he said, looking at Rebecca. 'All talk, no fuck.' But he set about saddling his string of three camels, and tied my bag on to one of them.

I'd not had many dealings with camels before, for which I was soon grateful; my only knowledge of the beasts came from boxes of dates and Christmas cards. We're all familiar with the shape, of course, and it seems friendly enough: long neck, long legs, hump; silly face with long lashes and blubbery lips. But the Christmas card illustrators really fib: their drawings are about as accurate as the verses inside, the ones that say 'I wish you Merry Christmas cheer, And think about you all the year'; what the illustrators miss is the camels' attitude to life, which would make a hung-over bouncer with a grudge look like Mahatma Gandhi.

Rebecca and I stood aside as the Targui made retching noises, 'Hyhakha! Yakh! Myakhakhakh!' This could have been a reaction to the booze, but wasn't: the camels knelt. 'Do this way, yes please,' he instructed us, swinging into the saddle, crossing his legs and heaving on the rein. 'Byayacockacock!' The camel stood. Imrad sat, elegant and fierce, staring down at me, with one hand on the reins and the other on the pommel of a vicious curved sword.

I suppose from up there my own attempts with the camel must have looked pretty silly. He started to laugh as I made the attempt to climb into the saddle, which was fair enough because my camel decided to stand when I was only halfway on, leaving me sprawled across its neck and hump like a blanket-roll. But I did better than Rebecca. Or worse. She ignored Imrad entirely and kept a prudent distance from the beast he'd offered her.

'Is no!' called Imrad to me. 'Is no!' I had already worked this out.

He dismounted quickly and manhandled me on to my beast. 'Is better,' he assured me, and the camel stood. Rebecca, forced to choose between risking the camel on her own or having Imrad paw her on, chose the former. She made a better job of it than I had, and we were off. I quite like animals – dogs and cats and gerbils – the sort of animals you can go coochie-coo to without feeling an utter prat, but it's unlikely I'll ever get sentimental over camels.

Imrad led us on towards the border, talking to us all the time in his mixture of English and phlegm. 'This place is bandits, is famous, shuch! Is all bandits gone now though. Is good. Imrad met bandits, kill four, maybe five, was good. And here French patrol. Imrad kill French patrol here, kill four, maybe five, was good. Was '59, maybe 1960. Imrad led guerillas, ten men, two guns, took turns to fire guns till too hot to hold, pass to next man. See rock up there? Imrad led guerillas, attack other group, PFN, POUM, kill four, maybe five, in first gun burst, was good, kill four, maybe five, later. Was good.'

His conversation was mostly like this, but occasionally he told us Tuareg jokes. 'Is what is a tall dog?' he asked, supplying his own answer: 'An Arab!' Perhaps it was funnier in the original Berber. Imrad certainly seemed to enjoy it. He laughed heartily, and we laughed too because he knew where he was and had a big knife, and we didn't.

At least the camel gave me a chance to appreciate the landscape. From a distance the mountains were grey, flat grey; close to, they were shot with silicon and graphite, or something like that, and glistened, while the sun picked out pastel shades from the rocks and stone, shades that merged and blended softly and wildly like a riot of toilet rolls. The shapes were equally impressive: rough hard shapes, not carved by water like the British landscape; shapes that were broken off, honed by the heat, seared by the wind, forms that stretched and menaced above us. Most impressive of all though was the scale: the foothills rose straight from the desert, and the mountains rose straight from the foothills. Everything was fortification; nothing offered comfort.

There are problems in desert travel that – for reasons of taste – the average guidebook avoids mentioning. The sand gets everywhere, even there; the European stomach starts to slop about as a result of the nasty water and funny food; there's nowhere to have a shit except in a hole in the sand, which is awkward when you're in the rocks and even more awkward in mixed company; and you're all dehydrated anyway, losing pints of water through your skin, so though your stomach says you've got the runs your bowels disagree, which hurts. But enough of that. I won't mention it again; I just wanted to let you know.

For the first two days with Imrad we were alone, three travellers in a wilderness of vast leering rocks, and for the third we travelled with a group of Tuareg. The men were dressed much like Imrad, in blue and white, and rode their camels superbly; the women wore white, almost exclusively, with much jewellery and no veils. They were a handsome race. We rode with the women, and the whole party bivouacked together, but when we woke up the following morning all the Tuareg had gone, except Imrad.

Every so often my camel jostled close to Rebecca's. Our conversations were much the same at each opportunity; one of us asked where we were going and the other said they didn't know. Imrad was no help. Whenever we asked him where we were, he just grinned and winked his one eye. 'Trust me,' he said. He seemed to assume that we would follow him wherever he went, which was a pretty reasonable assumption, given that the alternative would be death. On the other hand neither of us fancied trogging round El-Hoggar till Doomsday at the whim of a Targui with a drink problem. But then, inexplicably, we were out of the mountains and in the open desert. The dunes here were regular, and rounded like buttocks; we passed between them like ants on a nudist beach. Judging from the fact that the sun came up on our right and set on our left, we were going north. It was the only clue we had.

The fourth night was spent at a water hole, surrounded by a tatty family of desert Arabs; Imrad treated them with disdain, and drew his sword to chase away their children. The children, sensibly, went.

By the fifth day I was used to the camel, after a fashion, but I was developing bad camel sores, and by the sixth day I was virtually standing in the saddle, which was causing a whole new set of problems. Rebecca, suffering equally, was almost lying on her camel's hump. It was a relief to see the border.

I hadn't expected the border to be so obvious – the rest of the desert was indistinguishable – but during the War of Algerian Independence it had been heavily fortified. We rode alongside row after row of crumbling concrete tank traps that were like regimental tombstones for the next war's dead, barbed wire that rambled and looped viciously, and abandoned pillboxes of crumbling concrete that exposed a net of rusting steel reinforcements. The French manage to make all their military ruins look like Verdun or the Maginot line: I expect it gives their generals a sense of nostalgia.

We followed the battered defences for a full day's journey north. El-Hoggar fell away behind us; we entered a vast and dusty plain, a sort of semi-desert, not as arid as the landscape we'd passed through, but pretty nasty for all that, with sharp grasses for company and the occasional thorn bush, and at the end of the day we slept.

It wasn't too uncomfortable, but I didn't like the area. The semi-desert lacked the harsh ochre and sky-blue beauty of the real thing; it was scrubby and dirty, made worse by the line of border fortifications, and in the morning sun the long shadows made the tank traps look even more like tombstones. We rode the seventh day in silence, concentrating on avoiding our saddle sores, and the plain gave way to low hills, partially covered with something like bracken and gorse, that reminded me, surprisingly, of Derbyshire or North Devonshire.

'Perhaps we are getting near the sea,' Rebecca said, for the hills looked like the dunes on a coast, but there was no sign of water.

The line of fortification had grown wider and more formidable now. Between the clumps of bracken there was sand, and between the fortifications were open spaces, patches of pasture dotted with the remains of dead animals. 'Minefields,' said Imrad. 'Been swepted at no time never.' We passed several such fields, some no more than a hundred yards square, others more than a mile long, and then Imrad called a halt. 'You want cross a minefield ever?' he asked. On my list of ambitions, crossing minefields was just below limbo-dancing under a moving lorry, but as my camel followed Imrad's wherever it went I didn't have much choice. We picked our way between the carrion-cleaned bones of another open space.

After death an animal breaks down gradually into smaller and smaller units – dust and dirt and amino acid chains. Rebecca's camel was impatient though. Rebecca's camel speeded this process up. We were halfway across the minefield when Rebecca's camel stepped on a mine and blew itself to smithereens.

TWELVE

The explosion was flat and ugly, then the sky was full of muck. This wasn't shit hitting the fan, it was a midden going through a turboprop, but at last it subsided. Like me, Imrad had been ducking to avoid the raining debris, but his reflexes were faster than mine. He had already turned his camel and was returning to the newly made hole while my camel was still bucking like my belly. By the time my beast had subsided Imrad was kneeling by the mess where Rebecca's camel had been; I took one look and my stomach was heaving again. God knows it was a depressing sight. The camel was still vaguely recognizable. There was a hump still, and a neck flat out on the ground, and the head twisted sideways with the lips nuzzling the soil, but the legs were shredded stumps splayed out at right angles from the body, and even as we watched the fatty hump was subsiding and sliding Rebecca's body on to the sandy grass. I have never seen anyone look half so dead. She was limp and lifeless, covered in blood and tissue, and a slime of viscera smeared out of her mouth; I was gagging so hard I could feel my balls in the back of my throat, and when she asked me to help her up I nearly bit the buggers off.

'Rebecca? Are you all right?'

She spat camel guts from her mouth. 'My camel must have absorbed the force of the explosion. Now give me a hand up, please.'

'Stay where you are,' I said, because it sounded the right thing to say. 'Don't move.'

She retained an impressive amount of dignity. 'If you think, Mr

Diamond, I am going to stay here with half a camel sprayed over me, you have another think coming.'

'No!' said Imrad urgently. 'He right. No move. Maybe other mine.'

'I thought you knew this minefield,' said Rebecca coldly.

'So I make mistake. Is okay for you. Not your fucking camel.'

Rebecca said something, probably something Hebrew, probably something uncomplimentary.

'What do we do now?' I asked. I was getting ever so diplomatic.

'How fuck I know?' asked Imrad in return. 'Mebbee wait, yes? You going to buy me new fucking camel?'

'What are we waiting for?' Now Rebecca was asking the questions.

'Is border. Army patrol, 'elicopters, someone come soon.'

The camel I was on was either bored with the standing around or distressed at the sight of its dead companion. It hoisted a hind leg belligerently, blew a characteristically obnoxious fart, and started to stroll back the way we'd come. This was so obviously a good idea that I felt almost elated. 'Follow me,' I called, and after a while they did, Imrad turning in the camel tracks and scooping Rebecca on to his camel.

When we reached the edge of the minefield again I called for my camel to stop, and after a hundred yards or so it did, turning round and rejoining Imrad and Rebecca. 'At least we're out of the minefield,' I said, feeling quite cheerful.

'Sure,' said Imrad, who was far from cheerful. 'In Qafadya though.'

'We'll just have to find another way through.'

'You got passport? You got big guns go'n' blast way through?'

'No.'

'In trouble is you. Hey, be getting off my camel. Don' wan' lose no more fucking camel.' He shouted something in Targui and the camel knelt. I climbed off. 'Leave you two here,' he announced, depositing Rebecca feet first on the ground. 'Should never listen to Major Fahd, no. He say meet you in mountains, okay, take you to border, no probballem, go cross minefield between withered tree' – he waved at an insignificant scrubby brush beside us – 'and line of hill over there. And what happen? Fucking camel fucking blown fucking bits, is what! I had enough. Am off.'

'Hey! What are we meant to do?'

'Walk.' He tugged at the reins of his camel and started to trot away.

'Wait!' I called.

He stopped, reluctantly. 'What now, eh?'

'You can't leave us here! We'll die!'

'Mebbee you lucky. Mebbee border patrol, 'elicopter find you. Mebbee Major Fahd he come lookin'.'

'We've got no water! Rebecca might be hurt!'

'I'm all right,' she said, but I disregarded her. I was staring at Imrad. I couldn't believe he was going to desert us like this. There were impotent tears forming in my eyes.

'Okay. I give you water. Then I go. I fuck off. My fucking camel I lost. How you like it, it your camel? No more doing nothing for Europeans, no way. I fuck off.'

He was genuinely upset. A tear, a different sort of tear to mine, rolled out of his one good eye and moistened the top of his veil briefly before evaporating. I tried to be of help. 'I lost a son once,' I said.

'Son! Fucking son! I lose a camel and you say son!'

Well, this was a fresh perspective. But he did unfasten a water bottle from the camel I'd been riding and toss it down at us, and did speak in a more friendly fashion. 'Okay,' he said. 'I tell you what. You go north, eh, follow border. You surely meet patrol. No problem. Okay. I go now. So long.'

And this time he went. We watched him, a tall figure riding high above the scrub, then climbing a ridge towards the bleaker dunes. We watched until he was out of sight. 'We're in trouble again,' she said.

'Never mind. We've got each other.'

'Is that a joke?'

'You tell me.' I put my arms out to her and held her by the shoulders. She neither resisted nor encouraged. I drew her closer. Still she made no move. I might even have kissed her – though by Christ neither of our lips were in any condition for kissing – except at that moment the helicopter swooped. And then the shadow crossed us, and we looked up.

The helicopter was a sort of dark blob in the sky with a pylon for a tail. It climbed away from us and turned, keeping diligently to the Algerian side of the border, we noted; its shadow had only crossed us because the sun was past its zenith.

'I expect he wants to know what we are doing here,' said Rebecca.

'If he finds out,' I answered, 'he can tell me too.'

We waved at the helicopter. It shifted a little in the air and flew towards us. Above the clatter of the engine an amplified voice called, first in Arabic and then in French, but the words were swept up by the rotor blades.

We waved again. The helicopter bobbed in the sky, as though avoiding a blow we could not see, and returned to the far side of the fortifications. 'Now what?' I asked. It circled a couple of times and landed in a cloud of dust; the engine was switched off, and the silence was a relief.

Two figures climbed out of the helicopter. They were a good quarter of a mile away across the minefield. One of them carried a gun, it seemed; the other carried something else. The something else turned out to be a megaphone, and the man carrying it called us again. The Arabic escaped me, naturally, but I caught some words of French. He was asking us to identify ourselves.

'Can't we mention the Cairo Accord?' I asked. 'It kept us alive in Qafadya.'

'It would not work here. These men are soldiers, not intelligence men. They would not have heard of the Accord.'

'Then perhaps we could tell them the truth. We were hijacked and we're trying to get out of Qafadya. We'd better mention Imrad too, tell them our guide was scared off. They'll have seen the remains of the camel on the minefield.'

'The Algerians are not particularly sympathetic towards hijack victims,' she warned me.

'They're probably not enthusiastic about Irish terrorists or Israeli spies either. At least as victims they've nothing against us.'

She shrugged and called back a stream of Arabic; the man with the megaphone pantomimed cupping a hand behind his ear. 'He can't hear us,' she said. 'We'll have to go closer.'

Once again we followed our tracks through the minefield, releasing an updraught of flies when we reached the smashed camel. We followed the tracks to their furthest limit, stopped, and Rebecca repeated her lines of Arabic.

There was much consultation among the Algerians as they heard our story, much shrugging and waving of hands, and then they returned to the helicopter.

'Do you think they believed you?'

She shrugged. The engine started again and a swirl of dust was raised as the blades turned; the helicopter rose out of the dust and hovered overhead.

'Next?' I wondered aloud.

Next was a rope ladder that dropped from the helicopter. The ladder was maybe thirty feet too short. A figure hung from a leg of the craft and waved the pilot down, but as it came lower its blades started disturbing the sand. The hanging man shouted something. 'He says catch the ladder!' translated Rebecca, virtually screaming over the noise of the engine, but it was still out of reach.

The pilot brought it lower. I could just make out the helicopter's shape, and the trailing ladder, but all around me was a swirl of dirt. Then the ladder, dragging its last few rungs, swept into my reach, and I grabbed it. 'Climb up!' I shouted to Rebecca.

My eyes were full of grit and I could barely keep them open. I hung on to the ladder and felt Rebecca take hold too. The weight shifted as she climbed. I tried to look up, to see how high she had gone, but here in our private sandstorm there was nothing to be seen. I was choking.

As she climbed Rebecca altered the balance of the helicopter. The rope lurched in my hands. I just kept my grip but a second tug jerked the air from my lungs, and when I filled them I filled them with sand. I choked and let go, and the helicopter, delicately balanced on its column of air, must have suddenly lifted, for when I grabbed the ladder again I realized I was holding the very bottom rung.

As the helicopter rose the dust storm settled. I looked down. The whirlwind had cleared a large circle of sand, exposing the dull metal casings of several mines. Then the helicopter dragged me a couple of feet off the ground and started to pull me left. Rebecca, fifteen feet above me, was hanging on with arms and legs; all I had to hang on with were my hands. I touched ground again, running comically half-on, half-off the sand as I was pulled further left, then losing my footing as the machine dropped a little. I was being dragged entirely now, on my knees and thigh, and the burnous was unwinding itself, making movement even harder. Through my gritty eyes I saw a mine the helicopter had revealed. It was close and getting closer as I was towed toward it.

The helicopter dropped lower still. Maybe the pilot wanted to help me get my footing but my burnous was too much of a mess and I just collapsed on to my chest. I suppose I should have let go the ladder, but I didn't: I just let the helicopter pull me nearer and nearer the mine. I saw, terrifyingly close, its riveted rim and squat central trigger. My head actually passed it and my shoulders brushed it. I tried to pull myself up the ladder to avoid making contact, but my knees still came at the trigger. I kicked down with both bound legs, hopping upwards like a flea, and got over it, my foot catching its edge. As I watched, horrified, the mine reared up, balanced, and slowly toppled over.

Suddenly I was on my way up. The pilot must have seen my danger. The land fell beneath me at a rush. The mine was on its edge above the hole like a headstone, and then falling.

The explosion sent me spinning across space. I clung desperately to the ladder. I wanted my eyes shut but they stayed obstinately open, so that I was watching as I shot upwards to the same level as Rebecca, yo-yoed back down and swung wildly. The helicopter dropped back down, and I knew I'd no fight left in me, so I surrendered my body to the inevitable destruction.

But nothing happened. We were clear of the minefield. I collided with a sharp, spiny bush, let go of the ladder, and collapsed into the yielding sand. Then there was an ugly pain in my shoulder, and I was still, dazed, and alive. Rebecca too dropped off the ladder as the helicopter dipped; she stumbled and fell heavily. Somewhere else, on the badly fortified border of my consciousness, the machine was landing in its tube of dust. The dust subsided; the soldiers, heavily armed, stepped out. We were under their guns. We were under arrest. But we were over the moon.

THIRTEEN

There was no room in the helicopter for us, so the pilot radioed for assistance. We lay in the shadow of his machine and our wounds were dressed. Rebecca had a twisted ankle that swelled as we watched; I had a suspected fracture of the collarbone. We had been lucky: five days in the desert, two landmines, no shoes, and still to be among the living was an achievement.

The second helicopter was not long coming. It was a Westland, the sort the Brits use for Air-Sea Rescue. The Westland is a very calm, respectable-looking machine, the sort that ought to smoke a pipe. It hovered and dropped noisily.

There were stretchers aboard, and we were strapped down and carried in. A doctor examined us briefly, pulling down the burnouses to check for bruising and exposing Rebecca's shapely breasts. I smiled at her.

'We must stop meeting like this,' she said, and then the doctor injected her with something that knocked her out. Her lips moved a little as she settled into sleep. 'You did OK . . . for an amateur.'

I looked at her and her breasts and made to reply, but she was gone. The back of a helicopter is no place to feel horny anyway; it's no place to feel anything. The doctor obviously agreed. I felt a sharp prick in my upper arm – no phallic jokes please – and there was nothing left to feel, just a hazy contentment that lasted mere seconds, and the next I knew I was in a small white room with the rotor blades of the helicopter turning and turning and turning into a ceiling fan. I had a drip in my arm, and there was a middle-aged nurse with dark skin sitting at my bedside. She was reading a novel in French, but I suppose I must have groaned or something, because she looked up, rested a fleeting hand on my shoulder, and left the room.

I sat up as best I could, with the memory of her touch still painful on my aching collarbone, and the drip hampering my movement. It was a cool, white room. The floor was polished slabs of grey stone; across from me was a sink where the taps had long handles like hygienic handlebars. Overhead the fan blades nudged the air at me, on the bedside table were my credit cards. They seemed to lead a charmed life: I could still prove my identity, if only by my debts. There was a large three-quarter length window to one side, and a view of dark trees with a spread of blue sky beyond. I sank back in the bed, trying not to jar the drip or my aching bones. A white seagull turned on its pointed wings against the blue beyond. It was nice here, wherever here was.

From the corridor there were voices. 'You get outa my way, heh. I'm an old friend. We're alla old friend.'

The second voice was English, and vaguely familiar. 'That's right. Now be a love.'

'We have diplomatic rights,' added a third voice, also English and very plummy. The nurse, outnumbered, let the delegation through.

'Isa this the guy?' asked the Italian.

I recognized the MI7 agent before he recognized me. But then I expect I'd changed during my journey through the desert, and he'd barely changed his socks. He came up and scrutinized the sun-seared face and the scrubby beard I'd grown in the desert. I smiled at him in a friendly fashion. 'Yes,' he said. 'It's him.'

The Italian was no more than thirty, short and stocky. Black hairs sprouted in the open neck of his shirt. His moustache was well groomed and romantic. His bottom was negligible and his stomach wasn't. He had a scar. In fact he was everything a Mafioso should be, except he wore no hat. 'Let's akill the fucker.'

'I hardly think that's necessary,' said the plummy voice, speaking through the mouth of an impressive Arab in flowing white robes. I liked him. He didn't want me to die.

'Why wait, heh? He's a gonna. He's a gonna die.'

'Please, Mr Lamotti,' said my English friend. 'We have questions to ask him.'

'Ashoota first, ask questions after,' muttered the Italian. And yes, I know he sounds like a stereotype, a caricature; he was a bloody caricature, and it made him no less dangerous.

'Mr Thorpe is quite correct,' said the Arab. I didn't know any Thorpe but presumed he meant the MI7 man, the man I knew as Chambers. 'Besides, any unfortunate incident might endanger my diplomatic status. Both personally and as a representative of the embassy I should be highly embarrassed by a precipitate act of violence.' He paused, presumably for breath. 'I would recommend we remove him from the hospital and, at our leisure, dispose of him without incriminating ourselves or our friends in any way.' I was going off this bloke already.

I was also getting tired of being treated like I wasn't there, so I lifted myself up, with my broken collarbone creaking. 'Just hold it a . . .' I began, but the Italian, Lamotti, cut me off with the back of his hand on my mouth. 'Shut it!' he said. Thin blood dribbled through my teeth and beard, dripping on to the clean linen. I ran a tentative tongue round my mouth. 'Let'sa go!' said Lamotti. He was almost a joke and, like most of my jokes, wasn't funny. He was also the youngest and least dignified of my visitors, for even poor old Chambers had a sort of downtrodden, worn-out dignity, yet he was in charge; I guess they were playing a nasty game and he was nastier than the rest. 'Let'sa get him out of here.'

'It won't be cheap,' said the Arab. 'The Algerians are not a corrupt people. The price will be high.'

'Bigman will pay. It'sa he awants this punk.'

'I don't mean the price in money,' said the Arab. 'I mean the price in prestige. I'll have to ask it as a favour from my embassy.'

'Fuck your prestige an' your precious embassy. Just sort it out, heh.'

The Arab looked at Lamotti as if he had something to say, but he must have thought better of it, because with an angry glance he turned and left.

Chambers (or was it Thorpe?) looked through the window. 'Nice room,' he muttered, but if he was hoping to start a conversation he was out of luck. Lamotti was standing at the side of the bed, too busy looking intimidating to bother with small talk, and I was too intimidated. Time went by. I felt dizzy and sick so I leaned back on the pillow and closed my eyes. Who was 'Bigman'? I wondered.

At last the Arab returned with a couple of Arab porters and a doctor. Lamotti's mouth smiled at me while his eyes measured me up for my coffin. He made a pretence of scratching himself under his shirt and let me see the meaningful butt of the gun he wore in his armpit. Then the doctor injected me with something, and I returned to oblivion.

When I came to, I was sitting upright in a darkened room. A little sunlight creeping round the edges of the curtains dusted their dark green velvet with primrose yellow and provided the only light. There was a pressure at my wrists; I tried to move my hands and discovered, without surprise, that I was tied to the chair. This did not matter so much. Neither did the fact that I was still dressed in hospital pyjamas. The drug had left me woozy, almost content.

A sudden light snapped into my eyes. 'Back in the world of the living, are we?' It was my old friend Chambers. I winced and turned my neck to avoid the light. 'Sorry to be melodramatic, old boy,' he said, from the dark.

The interrogating light cast sharp shadows into the room. To the right was a fireplace, with the familiar portrait of General Tassat above the mantelpiece; to the left was a mahogany door in a carved frame.

'Look,' said Chambers, in a friendly fashion. 'Do you think you could manage a small favour? You're a dead man anyway; Lamotti's gunning for you and he doesn't strike me as the type to mess about. I want that book you were carrying. Actually I'm in a spot of bother.

By rights I should have got it from you in Djouarane but, well, one thing led to another and by the time I'd got in touch with Major Fahd you'd left for the border. I've been waiting for you here in Algiers for the past five days.'

'Algiers?' I cocked my head at the portrait. 'Aren't we in Qafadya?'

'We're in the Qafadyan embassy.' He didn't want to be sidetracked. 'Now, about that book.'

The book, however, was a problem. I'd forgotten all about the bloody thing. To the best of my knowledge it was still strapped to one of Imrad's camels. It seemed wiser not to tell him this. 'How important are you?' I asked.

'In what?'

'In all this.' I'd meant to give a wave to illustrate my point; I'd forgotten my hands were tied to the chair. 'In all these shenanigans.'

'Oh.' He hesitated. 'Very.'

'Tell me the truth.'

'Well, fairly then.'

'And you really work for MI7?' This claim had been bothering me. It was unlikely; it was so unlikely it might just be true.

The reply was evasive. 'Some of the time,' he admitted.

'What about now?'

He paused again. 'No.'

'So who are you working for?' I seemed to be leading the interrogation but what the hell, it'd be his turn later.

I expect he smiled at me through the dark, ingratiatingly. 'The same as you,' he said.

'What! Flaherty! INLA!'

'Well, not exactly. But my boss is Flaherty's boss.'

'Bloody Christ man! You mean Mulligan was right? Flaherty does work for the Brits?'

'Well, it's not exactly an official operation . . .'

'So what kind of operation is it then?'

'I think we're smuggling guns and drugs.'

'You think!'

'Everyone's very secretive. I only know as much as I do by chance. I'm a stringer. I'm on a retainer, working from Thessalonika; mother was Greek as a matter of fact. Every so often I get a little job, tailing, that sort of thing. And they told me to tail you.'

'"They"? You're not talking about MI7?'

'I'm talking about Bigman.'

'Oh.'

'Anyway, I don't think even Bigman expected you to get hijacked, because I got a phone call from him, in person, sending me to Qafadya.'

'To meet me?'

'To identify the body, actually,' he said, embarrassed. 'But, well, opium has always been a vice of mine. Have you ever tried it? It's the white nights I love, when there's no light yet everything is light and you lie on your bed completely at ease.'

'Get on with it.'

'Nothing else to say. I should have got the book off you and I failed. That's all there is to it.'

'So now's your second chance.'

'That's right.'

'Who's Lamotti?'

'He's a thug. Runs Bigman's operations in these parts.'

'And he's going to kill me?'

'That's right.'

'That's a pisser.'

He was even more embarrassed now. 'I'm afraid it is,' he agreed. Then his voice perked up. 'There's no need to make it a massacre though. Hand over the book and at least he won't murder me.'

'Ah. There's a bit of a problem there. I haven't got it.'

'But you know where it is?' He sounded more eager than worried.

'Approximately. It's somewhere in the Sahara desert.'

'Lost?' Now he was more worried than eager.

'Tied to the back of a Tuareg camel.'

Chambers came round to my side of the light. He peered at me with watery eyes, looking for the truth, and accepted, unhappily, that he'd found it. 'Now, that really is a pisser,' he said.

His weakness made me strong. I had an idea. 'Does Lamotti know what you want the book for?'

'Even I don't know what I want it for. I just do as I'm told.' He sounded peevish.

'Tell Lamotti you're taking me to England with you.'

'I can't go to England.' His face was still close. There was a curious smell on his breath – peppermint and gin and tobacco. It mingled in an odour of sweet decay.

'Take me anywhere,' I said expansively. 'Anywhere Lamotti isn't.'

He thought. 'I don't know if I could convince him. He didn't strike me as the reasonable type.'

'We've got nothing else to try.'

He stood up, out of the light. 'I'm out of my depth,' he said, more to himself than me.

That made two of us, but I didn't want to discourage him. 'I'm putting two and two together,' I said.

'And making?'

'I'm not sure. It's complicated. Have you heard of the Cairo Accord?'

'No.'

'It's a sort of international terrorist organization. A bit like Interpol, if I've got it right, but the other side of the law of course.'

'Ah well,' said Chambers, consigning the Cairo Accord to that place where insoluble worries, death and taxes are sent. 'Nothing much we can do about it. I wonder if Lamotti can be fooled, though. I don't think he's much more than a thug.'

'Where's Rebecca?' I asked.

'Ah, the floozie you were with in the desert. Still in hospital, I expect.' He smiled, a curious, almost cheerful smile for a man about to be killed by Lamotti. He was a simple bloke, I was learning, and not the sort to be pessimistic for long. 'That reminds me of a curious coincidence. I won't be long.'

He left the room. I sat in the chair, my arms tied and my collarbone aching horribly. General Tassat stared down at me like a benign vulture.

Chambers wasn't long. 'Thought this might interest you,' he said, tossing a magazine on to the table in front of me. It was a glossy magazine. The title was *Naughty Ladies*, but the subtitles on the cover seemed to be in Italian. Between the subtitles was a picture of a buxom girl in a mortarboard, gown, and nothing else. The gown hid rather than displayed her qualifications.

'Aren't you going to read it?'

'I'm tied to the bloody chair.'

Chambers turned the pages for me. 'It's just a little curio I picked up,' he said. 'But I was sure you'd be interested.' Inside were more pictures, with short Italian texts. There seemed to be a story. The setting was a girls' school. A schoolmistress with a bun and glasses told off the well-endowed girl from the cover. The girl, better dressed than she had been, wore a gym slip and a jaunty straw hat. Chambers turned to the next page. The girl was bending over and the teacher waving a cane. Big surprise – the girl's knickers were round her knees and her buttocks pouted at the camera with glossy bland unnaturalness, like a tulip. He turned the page again. At cane point, the girl was unbuttoning her gym slip and letting it fall to the floor, then standing there – no knickers, nice knockers – with her hands over her secrets and her breasts hanging out of an unlikely black basque. In that warm room I felt warmer, felt dew under my arm, but I can't say I was too involved. Under different circumstances I might have been aroused, but with my collarbone bust, my hands tied to the chair, and Chambers watching my face with a curious and disturbing intensity, self-abuse wasn't really on.

By the next page the girl had nothing on at all. She was a big girl. She was a very big girl. Her rosy boss-eyed nipples squinted at the teacher. She held out her hand and the teacher – for reasons perhaps explained in the text – handed over the cane. Another page was turned. Now it was the teacher's turn to undress, and while the plot escaped me the actions were easy to follow. Beneath the cool dove-grey dress and the mortarboard was a tanned body, sleek, smaller-breasted than the pupil's but just as alluring, and I was so busy looking at the allure, at the full-lipped smile between her legs, that it wasn't until two pages on, when the teacher let down her hair, that I noticed the face.

I gawped.

'Thought you'd be interested,' said Chambers.

For staring out of the page, her seductive tongue peeking through her teeth and her pussy opened to show the cowled tip of her clitoris and the dewlapped slit beneath, was Rebecca.

Fourteen

There didn't seem a lot of point dwelling on it, but I couldn't help feeling let down, and then feeling hypocritical. I felt let down because I had grown, what, let's say fond of Rebecca. I felt hypocritical because, had it been a complete stranger in the photographs, I'd doubtless have enjoyed the magazine. But Lamotti was a bigger problem, and I did my best to dismiss Rebecca from my thoughts.

'What were you meant to do with the book when I handed it over?' I asked. 'Give it to Lamotti?'

'No. He's the local capo, but from what he's been saying he knows very little about what's going on. He's like me, he just obeys the Bigman. I was to take the thing to Paris.'

'Paris?'

'There's an address I've been given, a hotel. I'm to meet someone there and hand the book over to him.'

'Is that all you know? Who's the man you're meeting?'

'He was described for me. Big man, grey-haired, early sixties, Irish. Calls himself Mahon. Mean anything to you?'

'The name doesn't: the description could be Flaherty's.'

'I thought Flaherty gave the book to you.'

'He did.' I pretended to think but knew I had too little to go on. 'Where are we now?' I asked, trying a different tack.

'The Qafadyan embassy in Algiers. Mohmet, the Arab you saw at the hospital, is cultural attaché here. He's all right, really, though scared stiff of Lamotti, of course.'

'Of course.'

We had been sitting together, as companionably as possible,

given that I was tied to a chair, for quite some time. But the tranquil mood was quickly changed. 'On your feet!' bellowed Lamotti. It sounded like 'Honour your feet' the way he said it, but as I was tied down I could obey neither instruction.

The Italian entered the room and waved his gun. Daylight burst in behind him, spreading a quadrilateral of light and a thug-shaped shadow across the carpet.

I shrugged as best I could with a broken collarbone, and smiled a weak hopeful smile I'd borrowed from Chambers. 'Sorry,' I said, though I wasn't sure what I was apologizing for. I just hoped to God he hadn't been listening at the door.

'Baaast!' he spat, and though I didn't know the word I got the sense. 'You gotta the book?' he asked Chambers, swivelling the barrel of his belly on him.

'Er. No. I don't need the book any more. Er. Mr Diamond will be coming with me to Paris, er, if that's all right. He can speak to Mr Mahon in person.'

'Hey. Now you awaita here one minute. Bigman's instructions, they was simple: you get the book, I kill the guy. Easy. Now you talking about taking the guy with you? Heh?' Lamotti revealed his teeth; Chambers' upper lip, scarred and scared, quivered.

'I'm sure Bigman would tell you . . .'

'Where the fuck you think we are? This is Algiers! This is my territory! I heard about your Bigman. Some English fucking nobleman. My capo he's met him. But this is *my* territory. Bigman don't tell me what to do, he ask. And he aska nice or he don't get.'

'Actually,' said a voice behind Lamotti, 'this is the territory of the Islamic Republic of Qafadya.' It was the cultural attaché, sounding suitably cultured. Behind him, in the corridor, was a bustle of soldiers in ochre uniforms. 'And loath though I am to question you in any way, Mr Lamotti, I have to tell you that were I forced to chose between listening to you and listening to Bigman I would listen to the latter every time.'

'What you telling me?' asked the Italian. 'You saying Lamotti,

go fuck youself? Is that what you saying? If that's what you saying
you dead, mister. Algiers ain't big enough to hide you.'

'All I am saying is that you should remember that, important
though you are in Algiers, and important though Algiers is in the
operation, you nonetheless depend on Bigman for a large pro-
portion of your business, as I do. Neither of us can afford to
antagonize him, least of all for the sake of a couple of nobodies.'

Fine. I was happy to be a nobody under these conditions. Or a
yes-body if that would serve better.

'Er,' said Chambers unimpressively. 'Perhaps I could . . .'

'Ain't no perhaps here!' said Lamotti. 'This is my town. You
justa remember, heh.'

The cultured attaché seemed more at his ease here than in the
hospital, and less vulnerable to Lamotti's bluster. 'I remember
perfectly well, Mr Lamotti. I remember that, in April last year, you
refused to hand over a consignment of Thai eighty per cent until
we raised the asking price. I remember that in June your men
interfered in the running of an Argentinian agent in Libya, and
threatened to give information to the CIA unless we gave you
greater control of the dockland operation. And I remember that as
recently as last month you personally killed two of our operatives
who, in your words, had been "in the way", severed their testicles,
filled their scrotums with thirty pieces of silver, and had them
delivered to the embassy here.'

'It's business,' said Lamotti, but the gun was indecisive in his
hand, wondering whether to worry Chambers or the Arab. 'Nothing
personal.'

The Arab smiled. 'Of course.' Very suave, very urbane. I was
getting fond of him again. 'Which is why, for purely business
reasons, you will find it expedient to put down that gun. I must
say, Mr Thorpe,' he said, addressing Chambers, 'your arrival in
Algiers was timely, and we will repay you with every assistance.
Our friend Lamotti has been a thorn in our sides for some time;
we had been seeking a way to get him into the embassy and your
quest to find Mr Diamond proved the perfect opportunity. Now,

Mr Lamotti, if you will be so good as to hand over your . . .'

Lamotti made a dive for the floor, firing his pistol. I thought the attaché had been pushing his luck – when a bullet took him in the neck I knew I was right. The Qafadyan soldiers stepped into the doorway and fired rapid bursts. I managed to throw myself and the chair to the floor and was grateful for the desk. Bullets rebounded.

When it was over, which did not take long, and when my broken collarbone stopped echoing to new bruises, which took longer, I looked up. From my position on the floor I could see Lamotti and the attaché. They were on the floor too. They looked less uncomfortable than me. They looked dead.

Feet in army gaiters walked between the corpses. A brusque, military voice spoke to Chambers in halting English, 'We assist? Yes?'

'That's – er – right,' said Chambers. 'We're going to – er – Paris.'

'Arrangements will be made.'

'Er – fine.' Despite all the 'ers', Chambers seemed to be getting what he wanted. Light flooded the room suddenly as the soldiers opened the curtains.

He bent close to me. 'Did you hear that?' he asked in a low voice. He was wheezing.

I nodded.

'Yippee!' he whispered in my ear.

I was getting used to Qafadyan efficiency. By the following morning we had climbed into a black Mercedes with blackened windows and were driving down the wide colonial-style road in the embassy district towards the airport with our fake passports in our hands. Chambers wore his customary grubby suit; I was much smarter in a European suit the cultural attaché wouldn't be needing any more, with his tight shirt open at the neck and his shoes pinching my feet.

When we passed the Italian embassy a large Peugeot pulled out behind us. It followed us the twelve or so miles out of town to the airport, winding along white roads that climbed through citrus groves. The sun was bright overhead. Lamotti had been Italian; I hoped the Peugeot had nothing to do with him. But there was nothing to be done. I looked out at the view. The coast of Algeria, the Algerian Riviera, is as lovely as anywhere on earth. Maybe this beauty explained why the French had struggled so long and so hard to retain Algeria; I couldn't explain the Brits' presence in Ulster that way. Poor unlovely Ulster. As we climbed out of the town and over the headland, with the patient Peugeot still on our tail, the sun stroked the waves in the curving blue sea, and boats plied their way through the waters. The ship Rebecca and I were to have taken would be down there somewhere.

The CD plates on the car made access to the airport easy. The Algerian police politely waved us through, and the car on our tail. Our driver said something to us in Arabic; Chambers translated. 'He says to stay in the car.'

The car was comfortable. I was happy to wait, and watch the Peugeot. The Peugeot seemed happy to watch us. This could have gone on for some time. 'How long before our plane comes?' I asked.

'Two hours.'

I sat back on the comfortable upholstery. My hand went inside my jacket and I fingered the passport in my inside pocket. That and my credit cards were all I had, and the cards had become a sort of touchstone. Outside the Peugeot reflected the sun, and Chambers and I studiously avoided mentioning it. A plane came in, a sleek but old-fashioned 727, landing tidily on the hot runway.

The driver stepped out to open our door. I looked across at the Peugeot. Sure enough, its doors were opening too. Chambers and I walked across the tarmac towards our plane. I could feel eyes on us; Italian eyes, steeped in vendetta and revenge. We climbed the steps of the plane. At every step I winced as my broken collarbone jarred and imaginary Mafia bullets smashed into my back. Chambers walked as stiffly as I did.

Suddenly there was the sound of feet rattling up the metal stairway behind us. 'Don't turn round,' said Chambers, so I did.

I'd expected Kalashnikovs so seeing Rebecca was one hell of a relief. 'What are you doing here?'

'Just keeping an eye on you.' She smiled at me from behind dark glasses, then climbed aboard and handed her suitcase and passport to the stewardess. Like mine, her passport was Swiss. She smiled at the coincidence and tossed her dark hair. 'Algerian forgers lack originality,' she said.

'I thought you were some mate of Lamotti's out for revenge,' I said. 'What were you doing at the Italian embassy?'

'The Italians handle Israeli affairs in Algeria. We've never had official representation here.'

My seat was next to Chambers. He leaned over and grumbled in my ear. 'What's she got to do with this?'

I explained briefly. Chambers was unhappy. 'For goodness sake!' he muttered when I'd done. 'You mean she's a professional! Can't you get rid of her?'

'I don't honestly see how.'

'I don't like it,' said Chambers. 'Bigman won't like it.'

'Then Bigman'll have to do something about it. We can't.'

'We'll give her the slip in Paris.'

I sat back in the seat. I was getting fed up with all this intrigue. I was tired and I wanted to go home. But there was no way out.

'One thing though.' It was Chambers, leaning over me confidentially again. 'This Major bar Hilai. I do like her cover!'

It was a long flight on a slow plane. As diplomats we were given first-class accommodation; as whites we were given first-class treatment. There were few whites on board. Most of the passengers were Algerians, and Algerians are the Catholics of France. I've always been a Catholic, an Algerian, a Nigger. I was not used to being a Prod, being one of the master race. I looked across the aisle at Rebecca, apparently snoozing behind her dark glasses, and thought about the mess in Palestine. The lesson persecution teaches isn't tolerance, it's how to persecute most effectively.

We flew north, into colder, more temperate, skies. I'd forgotten what clouds looked like. Obese grey bulges obscured Paris. I'd expected to see the Eiffel Tower. Fat chance. We landed in the rain.

We were passed through customs without drama. One or two people looked at us of course. We were all the colour of mahogany, she was pretty, Chambers looked shifty and I wore a sling, so I'd have been suspicious if they hadn't.

There was a tall, slender, elegant man waiting for Rebecca. She said goodbye to us and went over to him. I looked at Chambers. 'How the hell do we give her the slip now?' I asked. 'She's gone.'

He didn't bother to reply.

We went outside and he hailed a cab, letting the first one go and getting in the second like they do in the movies. If I was a baddie I'd wait in the second cab every time. Chambers gave the address: 'Hotel Majestique, St Lazare.' I looked at my wrist in search of my lousy service station watch, but it was probably still in the back of Fahd's Land Rover and was no less use to me there. At a guess it was noon. We travelled through the unfamiliar city, beneath the unfamiliar cloud, and the taxi pulled up, double-parking in a busy street.

The Majestique was a cheap, peeling hotel. In the window boxes were dead plants that shuffled in the breeze. A striped faded awning hung over the street. It shielded chipped plastic-coated furniture and plastic-coated tablecloths held in place by plastic-coated wire. Chambers paid the taxi and we went in.

'Is Mr Mahon about?' he asked at the desk.

'M. Mahon? One moment.' The clerk dialled a number on an incongruously modern telephone that was kept beneath the lip of the Second Empire desk. 'Excuse? Two gentlemen for you, M. Mahon.'

He looked at us questioningly. 'It's M. Thorpe,' said Chambers. 'And M. Martinu,' I added, giving the unlikely name on my new passport.

There was a pause, and then the voice at the other end of the line said something squeaky, which is the way voices at the other end of lines always speak, and the clerk nodded at me. 'Room 304.'

There was an antiquated lift which ran up the middle of the stairwell. I pressed the button to call it and it juddered into noisy action. When the lift reached us I had to open both the outer and inner gates which worked in concertina-fashion. I pressed for floor three and forgave it the long clanking wait. If I was to survive to the lift's age, which let's be honest isn't likely, I'd want to get my breath back too. There was a malicious and completely unforgivable lurch. Then we were under way. It would have been quicker to walk.

Through the mesh we watched the floors go by. The burgundy carpet was drab and threadbare, worn badly in the centre of each tread. We clattered up, past the half-landings that marked each floor: the first with its heavy reproduction commode; the second where the carpet changed for a cheaper dark blue one, even more badly worn; and the third where the feet were. The feet led up to legs and the legs led to torsos and arms and guns. 'We've got you covered,' said an Irish voice that bit at the syllables and chewed them before spitting them out.

'Flaherty?' I asked. The lift jerked and ground to a halt. The door was opened by one of the terrorists and it was Flaherty himself who stood before me. I noted with satisfaction that his fingernails were still blue and ugly-looking from the bite of my loyal ironing board.

'I presume you'll be Thorpe,' Flaherty said to Chambers before turning his attention to me. 'But who are you? And who sent you?'

'You did, you stupid Irish pillock!' I told him. 'Don't you recognize me? Jack Diamond, returned from afar.'

'Jack Diamond!' He looked through the tan and the new beard. 'Is it truly yourself? And what's happened to your arm?'

'It's a long story.' One of the gunmen opened the lift doors, and I stood there in all my glory like a present just unwrapped.

'You'd better be telling it all the same,' said Flaherty. 'I've still the same guns trained on your belly I had before. Frisk them!'

'You haven't changed,' I said, while one of his gunmen patted

me intimately in all the likely places and then one or two unlikely
ones.

'In my business you don't change, you just adapt. And now, if
you'll just say what you've got to say. Last I heard you'd been
hijacked by the Palestinians. You've brought the book?'

The question was aimed at Chambers rather than me;
Chambers, intimidated by Flaherty's rough manner and the guns
trained on his belly, was saying nothing.

We were ushered from the lift to a nearby door and shown in.
'Sit down, Jack, Mr Thorpe,' said Flaherty, sounding more friendly,
and we did. Flaherty sat astride his chair like John Wayne. 'Your
plane crashed in the desert,' he said conversationally. 'What did
you do, find a flying carpet?'

'Something like that,' I agreed. 'Are your heavies indoctrinated
in the you-know-what?'

'The you-know-what? What are you talking about?'

I gave Flaherty a pitying smile, the sort of smile I was going to
regret later. 'One across – Capital of Egypt, five letters. Four down
– Article with rope for agreement, six.'

He worked it out quickly, turned to the heavies, and waved them
from the room. 'All right,' he said when they'd gone. 'You owe me
an explanation.'

I owed Flaherty nothing but spoke just the same. 'Qafadyan
intelligence organized my trip to Algeria, and from there I travelled
on a Swiss passport.'

He dismissed me and turned to Chambers. 'Bigman told me
your brief was to bring the book. I don't recall asking for Jack
Diamond.'

'I've made a number of influential friends,' I told him, speaking
for Chambers, which wasn't hard as he wasn't speaking at all.

'Such as?'

I looked at him archly. 'I'm not sure that *you* have been indoctrinated into those particular secrets.'

I was going to pay for that later too. 'Cut the crap, Diamond,'
said Flaherty. 'You know nothing.'

'I know enough,' I said. 'I know about the Cairo Accord, and I know about the Englishman who's behind it, the one they call Bigman.' I lowered my voice further. 'I don't think the INLA boys would like it if they knew you were leading them up a gum tree for the sake of an English aristocrat.'

Flaherty, to give him his due, made a brave face of it. 'Unsubstantiated rumours.'

'Unsubstantiated when Mulligan threw them at you in my Kilburn flat, but hardly unsubstantiated now. You've heard of Major Fahd?'

'Qafadyan secret service.'

I nodded, and moved on in the conversation. 'Mr Lamotti?'

'No.'

'Personal friend of a personal friend of Bigman. Head of the organization in Algiers. I'm sure he'd back up my story.' Okay, so I was lying.

'What's to stop me having you two shot right now?'

'Two things. One is that I might just manage to persuade your boys to hear me out before they pulled the triggers, in which case you'd be the one catching the bullets in your balls. I might not manage that, I'll agree, but on the other hand I might, and you know me, Flaherty, I've always been a gambling man.'

'And the second?'

'I've still got the book. You haven't. And you still want it.'

He laid back on his chair. He was not a well man. The flesh around his eyes had a dull-yellow bruised tint, and the veins on his nose made a map of ill-health. 'What are you telling me?' he asked.

'I'm telling you that I have the upper hand.'

He clamped his teeth resolutely together and folded his arms. 'Your da's not going anywhere,' he reminded me. 'One word from me and he's dead. A second word and he'll be just wishing he was. The boys always like a bit of practice – shit!'

He sounded so distressed I thought for a moment he had. 'What's up?'

'Have you seen the bloody time? It's your stupid fault, Diamond. I've got the most important meeting of my life coming up and I'm going to miss it because of you.'

He was up and slipping into his brown overcoat before I could gather my thoughts. He looked down on me and clicked his fingers; the gunmen came back in, circling us like sharks. Flaherty turned away from me and raised his left arm from the shoulder. I saw the blow coming. It made no difference. Sickeningly, his elbow caught me square on the nose. I crumpled, and he bent over me. 'Two things,' he whispered, his voice in my ear. 'First, you'll not be saying anything for a day or two by the time I'm done. And second, next time you speak to me like that I'll break your fucking neck. Got it?'

I shook my head. Blood from my nose splashed my sling.

'Flaherty's working fo . . .' I started to say to the gunmen. The next blow was a chop to the back of the neck. I slumped off the chair and landed in a heap at Flaherty's feet.

'I don't think we quite heard you,' said Flaherty, concerned.

'Flaherty's wor . . .' Again I saw the blow coming. Again it made no difference. His boot smashed into the side of my face and then I knew no more.

When I came to, the three heavies were still in the room, sitting on the bed, fretfully cleaning their guns or tapping their feet. I couldn't see Flaherty, but Chambers, looking worried, was leaning over me. The curtains were drawn, but the quality of light was very different from the heavily draped room in Algiers. The curtains here were thinner, and the light beyond was less intense. Every so often one of the heavies went over and looked out of the window, carefully. It was daylight outside. I wasn't sure it was the same day.

'What's happening?' I asked. It was the third time I'd swum up from unconsciousness in as many days: it's usual, when you go down for the third time, to drown.

One of the heavies started at my voice, dropping a spring from his half-stripped gun. 'Christ, Diamond. We'd forgotten you was there.'

'Where's Flaherty?' I asked.

'He's fucked off out, hasn't he,' said a different heavy. 'I guess a lot's happened since he done your face for you.'

'Like what?' Chambers was shaking his head in a you-don't-want-to-know way.

'Like we're surrounded by plain-clothes dicks. Flaherty went out about two hours ago. He hasn't come back, but the constabulary has turned up. There's a carload of them out in the street, half a dozen along the corridor, and some more in the building opposite.'

'What are they doing?'

'Waiting. Same as us.'

A second heavy spoke: 'And what's become of Flaherty, I want to know?'

'Maybe the garda grabbed him as he was coming back,' said the first.

'Maybe. And maybe he turned us in. Pretty fucking convenient for him, isn't it: he goes out and we get surrounded.'

It was. 'Particularly when you consider he was in the pay of the Brits,' I said.

'The Brits!'

'A Brit,' I amended.

'There's a guy climbing up on the roof there!' said the third heavy, before any questions could be asked.

'Give me a gun!' I said.

'What d'you mean?'

'What's it sound like I mean? Give me a gun! Flaherty's no friend of mine – just look at my bloody face. And he's no friend of yours if he set this lot on to you. We might as well fight it out together.'

'All right.' Someone handed me a gun, a Kalashnikov with a wooden stock. 'I'm Pat by the way. This is Mick, and Paddy.'

'Pleased to meet you. I'm Jack, Jack Diamond. This is Mr Chambers. He's all right.'

'Call me Frank,' said Chambers.

'You wanting a gun too?' asked Mick.

'A pistol, perhaps,' said Chambers.

Pat was still looking at me. 'We'd heard you was dead,' he said.

'The report was premature,' I told them, and smiled as best I could.

'Let's keep it that way,' said Pat, and he didn't bother to smile.

FIFTEEN

The siege of the Hotel Majestique began without me; had I been given a choice it could have carried on that way, but I wasn't and it didn't. I held the Kalashnikov in my hand. It was a long time since I'd carried a gun. I'd hoped that it would feel familiar, that my early INLA training and my recent experiences would combine to turn me into an effective fighting machine. Instead I felt like throwing up, my buggered nose hurt like hell, dragging on my eyes and making them ache, and I was pretty sure that if I fired the gun the vibrations would tear my collarbone apart again.

Thriller writers have a phrase they think creates tension: 'We waited for what seemed like a long time.' We waited in the Hotel Majestique for what seemed like a long time, and then for what really was. Crepuscular French dusk slopped around the neighbourhood, pierced with whistles and motor scooters. In a nearby room a tranny bawled out pap music. And nothing happened, more than once.

I was getting tired. My Algerian convalescence had been screwed up; the past few days I'd been unconscious as often as conscious; Flaherty had added his blows. I dreaded to think what kind of mess my face would be in, and if I hadn't had more pressing worries I'd have worried myself sick.

Paddy, Pat and Mick were passing round roll-ups. I took one but my nose made it surprisingly hard to smoke: I like to send each expelled drag on its way with a puff of smoke from my nostrils. I'm not a heavy smoker, but I do enjoy a cigarette now and then; the fag was burnt halfway down, when there was a flurry of smashing glass and a smoke bomb was lobbed through the window.

Paddy acted fast. The bomb was lodged behind the drawn curtains and so far most of the smoke was escaping through the broken window. Paddy took advantage of this, picked up the bomb in the antimacassar off my chair, and dropped it back out of the window. As he ducked behind the curtain the machine-gun opened up.

The curtain lurched with Paddy's weight, bulged like a pregnancy, and then bore him into the room. He was cut to ribbons, with half his chest missing. The bullets had gone through him and the curtain and were bouncing round the room.

'I'm getting out!' cried Pat from the open doorway. He lifted his Kalashnikov and fired a palsied burst. 'You coming?'

'I'm with you!' affirmed Mick.

'And you?' Pat called to me.

'Right behind you,' I lied.

The two gunmen stepped into the hall, firing indiscriminately in the raucous rhythm of death. The door swung open behind them uninvitingly. Bullets ripped into the hinges, into the woodwork around it, into Pat and Mick. Mick staggered towards me. A bullet had passed through his neck. He fountained blood between clenched teeth, stared nowhere, and fell. I didn't see what happened to Pat. A battery of bullets had lifted him bodily and shooed him down the corridor out of sight. I sat still, and wondered what was going to happen next. Chambers sat with me. Neither of us had fired a shot.

We needed time to think. Did the police know we were in the room? That we were armed? That we were useless? Without really knowing whether there was any point we looked round for a hiding-place. Under the bed was too obvious. In the wardrobe ditto. The Majestique was an old-fashioned hotel, and even the modernizations were antediluvian. The large open fire had been replaced with a gas fire in a hardboard surround. We looked at one another. If we could get behind the hardboard we'd be concealed.

We worked at it quickly. The hardboard was held in place

crudely, stuffed behind angled nails. We needed to get it loose without scraping off too much incriminating paint.

There were people in the corridor now. I recognized official voices and official words: *'Mort'*, *'les terroristes'*, *'par example'*. Our fingers fumbled with the board. We prised it loose, struggled over the bloody gas fire, and squeezed tightly into the fireplace. We'd never have fitted in at all if we hadn't been in such a panic. The big question was whether we could get the hardboard back into position, and the straight answer was no. We were just arriving at this conclusion when the door opened.

I pulled at the sheet of hardboard, gripping it round the ill-fitting edges with my finger-nails. I was not at all comfortable. I was not about to be entombed in a slip road on the M25 but I was not at all comfortable. I was bent double. My fingers stretched to breaking-point as I tried to hold the board. A steady trickle of soot was running down my neck. And Chambers was sitting on my knee.

And then, strangely, things got boring. Or at least, as boring as they could, given that degree of discomfort. You want to know how boring? Imagine reading a Hungarian Do-It-Yourself manual in a two-foot square launderette. With Chambers breathing up your nose. I think I went numb.

Eventually the police must have decided it was safe to come in. We heard heavy dragging. Paddy and his curtain, I supposed: Paddy in his crimson shroud. French words, conversation and exclamation, flickered round the room like a shadow. *'Voilà'*, *'aussi'*, *'maintenant'*, were words that had stuck from my infrequent schooldays, when even my English vocabulary was limited. I tried to make out what was being said – what was left of my life might depend on it – and failed.

There was another boring interlude. The room beyond the fireplace sounded empty now. My fingers grew more and more numb. So did Chambers; he was virtually rigid. Without exchanging a word we decided, mutually, we'd had enough. We hadn't heard a word from outside for a long time. Gently I eased the hardboard from the opening, forcing it silently out of the fireplace. I put an eye to the crack, and the joker on the other side jammed his gunbarrel in my face.

A set of hairy fingers forced themselves into the gap and prised the hardboard off. Wearily, stiffly, Chambers and I climbed out of the hole. We weren't so much resigned to capture as grateful, I think. With much prodding, the policeman shoved us towards the lift.

I don't know if it was deliberate; I don't think it was. Just as we were getting into the lift Chambers fell backwards, knocking the gendarme's hand. The gun went off, the bullet shooting harmlessly upwards, and the policeman cursed. Another thing I don't know is what prompted me to run, but I did, going up the stairs two at a time. I heard the policeman curse again, and saw him raise his gun through the cage of the lift shaft. I ducked as he fired, and the bullet must have missed. I was virtually on my hands and knees but I was still sprinting up the stairs, spiralling round so I was directly over Chambers and the gendarme.

The policeman had an obvious problem: should he chase me or stay with Chambers? He settled for a compromise, and tried to force Chambers up the stairs with him, but like most compromises it was the worst of both worlds. Meanwhile he had shoved his whistle between his lips and was blowing like a kettle.

I got my breath and wondered why the hell I'd run. But it was too late to give myself up now: the policeman would shoot me on sight. So I carried on climbing, trying to keep Chambers and the policeman directly below me as we spiralled, which worked well till I got to the top.

I looked around hurriedly. I was on the service floor, and unlike the lower levels there was no corridor leading off, just a half-dozen cheap white doors. I tried each one but they were all locked. I tried forcing one. The cheap plywood gave after the third push and I found myself looking into a broom cupboard. There was no hiding-place there. Behind me I heard the machinery winching the lift. I turned and saw, at the top of the lift shaft, a sort of platform. It was odd I hadn't seen it before. I scrambled towards it. A small gate, fastened only by a bent nail, led me on to the platform. I climbed in and lay there, glad of the chance to breathe. Below me were more whistles now and, ominously, the sound of dogs slavering up the stairs. Then the lift machinery started to clank above my head, and I realized why I hadn't seen the platform earlier. It was the roof of the bloody lift.

I was travelling down. There was nothing I could do. I dropped slowly down the centre of the stairwell, past the policemen and their guns and dogs. I heard the bastards snigger as I went by.

The lift came to a halt at a lower floor, but I was still caged in, and though the gendarmes poked their sub-machine-guns through the bars and gestured at me, there was little I could do until I was taken back up to the roof. It was all so bloody ignominious.

I saw Chambers. He didn't look too much under arrest. In fact, he was laughing. 'Chin up, old man!' he called to me. 'Have you out in a jiffy.' I admit it: I raised two fingers at him, which only made him laugh some more.

And standing next to him, deep in conversation with a senior police officer, was Rebecca. I sat up and folded my arms. The whole thing was becoming a farce, and I was losing my sense of humour. At last I was being helped off the lift, only to be led down a single flight of stairs and back into it. I winced as it began to move; I'd had enough.

At the third floor, the scene of the siege, we stopped and got out. The police chief was trying to look serious though I'm sure he had been giggling at me; Rebecca made no such pretence. 'Jack,' she said, laughing prettily and showing off her small white teeth. 'You have a genius, you know that.' And then she looked concerned. 'But what has happened to your nose?'

I expect I scowled. They showed me back into Flaherty's room. The forensic scientists were now the centre of attention. The bodies were gone but where they had lain were white chalk sil-houettes, as sinister as corpses. Rebecca stood by my side. She was better dressed than me, which wasn't hard, in a tight red dress that showed off her curves, and despite her Saharan tan and the burns on her cheekbones and forehead still visible, she contrived to look very French and very glamorous. I comforted myself with the thought that her dress wouldn't suit me anyway. 'You have been lucky,' she said. 'I was reporting at the Sureté when the tip-off about the bombers came through. I guessed you might be involved. I managed to contact my opposite number in the SRSF, one of the French security services, and she arranged for me to come here.'

'You know who gave the tip-off?' I asked.

'I gather it was in English, and the man had an English accent.'

'An Irish accent, more like. I reckon Flaherty was behind this. It was even his way of working; he pulled off a similar trick in my flat not all that long ago.'

'I'm not sure,' said Rebecca. 'But I'm sure we will find out. The police record all incoming calls.'

We were taken back to the police headquarters. They asked for my statement. I gave it. They asked for it again. I gave it again. I was photographed from a number of angles like a convict. I asked for my nose to be cleaned up and the dressing on my arm to be replaced, and was ignored. Instead I was shown into another office and asked to give my statement for the third time. I felt like varying the story; I felt like maybe throwing in a few jokes. But the time for joking was over. In fact, had I been more sensitive, I would have realized the time for joking was over long before. So I went through my story once more, telling the truth, the whole truth, and nothing but the truth, or as near as I could manage, considering that I was in desperate need of a wash, a shave, a sleep, a bottle of brandy, forty cigarettes and a piss. They finally let me have the last.

They were especially interested in the notion that Bigman was an English aristocrat, and returned to this over and over again. But I had nothing to add. It was something Lamotti had mentioned and Flaherty hadn't denied.

After a lot of wrangling it was decided I should try to identify the recording of the tip-off. I kept telling them it was Flaherty who'd informed, and they kept smiling and shaking their heads. They sat me in a long steel-grey shoulder-scuffed corridor. They brought me a glass of water. Finally they took me to a small room with rubber egg-box walls. In the middle of the room was a lot of recording equipment and sitting behind it, twisting knobs like a connoisseur, was a fat gendarme. He played me the first seconds of the tape, drawing my attention to the slight clicking at the beginning of the call as the recorder had been activated, and the short-lived high peep that followed. Then came the message. It was terse and to the point. 'A group of Irish terrorists is planning a bombing campaign in Paris. They are staying in Rooms 304 to 308 in the Hotel Majestique, St Lazare. They are armed and trained. Maximum force is advised for their capture.' It was a distinguished voice, the sort of voice that gets what it wants, and I had never heard it before.

SIXTEEN

The way the French police were looking at me, I got the feeling I'd be lucky to make Devil's Island. I wasn't actually charged with anything, yet, but I had flown in from Algeria wearing a late Qafadyan diplomat's clothes and got myself involved in a terrorist shoot-out, and these, like 18-30 holidays, are the sort of things that give tourists a bad name. I hadn't taken a pot shot at the President or peed on Napoleon's tomb, but these were the only things to be said in my favour and I was shoved into a cell. The graffiti on the wall went back a while. 'Dreyfus is innocent.' I wondered what had happened to Chambers and Rebecca. I hadn't seen them since we got to the police station.

The cell looked out over a parade ground. The far wall was pitted and chipped by ancient bullets, souvenirs of earlier wars. I imagined seeing soldiers in black uniforms drag Rebecca across the yard, lean her against the wall, and kill her. She would be brave. Afterwards, Chambers would be led out. He wouldn't be. He would scream and offer betrayal, and they would accept, and kill him. It was pure fantasy, of course. Of course.

A man in a long raincoat came into the cell. I was hoping for Inspector Clouseau; I got Norman Tebbit in dark glasses. Everyone was wearing dark glasses; it was time I got myself a pair. His tight skin was stretched from his polished forehead, across his polished cheekbones, down to his polished teeth. I bet he sharpened those teeth at night. They were good teeth, and his English was good, and these were the only things about him that were. 'Mr Diamond,' he said, emphasizing the gap between the first and second parts of the word. 'I have been hearing interesting things of you. Very interesting.' I expected him to add 'But stupid.' He didn't. Maybe the accent was wrong. 'For instance, you have entered France on a forged passport. The forgery is undoubtedly the work of an Algerian Mafia cell. In France you have been involved in a shoot-out with the police. In the course of this shoot-out three terrorists were killed. Meanwhile we discover the head of the head, if you pardon the phrase, of the self-same Algerian Mafia cell. It is impaled on a spike outside a disreputable club in Algeria. In short, you murdered this Mafioso, fled Algeria, arrived in Paris, and were captured after a shoot-out. Yes?'

'No! It wasn't like that.'

He smiled, felt in his pocket, and drew out a packet of Gitanes; he tapped a cigarette against the box several times, put it in his mouth, and struck a flame from a petrol lighter. 'I know that.' He inhaled. 'And you know that.' He exhaled. 'But would a court believe such a thing?' The cell was softened with pale blue smoke, but this was no soft sell. 'The *Code Napoléon* has no time for such notions as "innocent before proven guilty"; in France, if we want your balls, we take your balls, and all you can do about it is scream.'

'If you know I didn't do those things, why accuse me in the first place?'

He took another drag on his cigarette. The loosely packed tobacco fizzled in the silence between us like electricity. 'Someone must be found guilty.'

I looked out at the courtyard. The clouds hung low over the gunshot-peppered wall. Every window was barred. The tricolour hung oppressively from a pole fashioned like a spear. '*Vive la France*,' I muttered under my breath.

The man came up behind me, staring at the view over my shoulder. For a moment he shared what I saw, and then he thumped me, twice, in the kidneys. The second blow felled me.

He stood above me, the cigarette hanging from his lip. 'You should not have said that. I do not like sarcasm.'

'You shouldn't have heard it,' I gasped.

He tapped his ash carefully on to my face. I winced and shook it off. Who was he? He said 'Tut, tut,' and bent over. He leaned close to me and inhaled on the cigarette. It glowed three times, once in his mouth and once in each lens of his dark glasses. I was suddenly glad of the glasses: I would rather the empty lenses than the empty eyes beneath. Then he took the cigarette from his mouth and placed it, delicately, against my cheek. I could feel the heat on the soft bristles above my shaving line. I tensed but stayed still, as though a wasp or worse were crawling on my skin.

'What do you want?' I asked.

'Are you frightened?'

'Terrified,' I assured him. 'You can stop now.'

I felt the scarlet glare as he burned me, and then the pressure was released. 'Not frightened enough,' he commented, wearily. The blind dark glasses looked at me steadily.

'Don't you believe it,' I said, sincerely, and felt the moisture down my trouser leg. He was a corrupt Tiresias who had seen it all.

'*Vive la France*,' he said, and I thought he meant me to repeat it after him. '*Vive la France*,' I agreed. But the dark glasses were looking elsewhere by now, and there was irony in his voice as he stood and spoke again. '*Vive la France*. Pah! France is dead.' He crushed the cigarette with a symbolic heel. 'It died at Sedan, at Verdun, at Vichy. It died in Indo-China and in Algiers.' He softened his voice. 'Especially,' he told me sadly, 'it died in Algiers. How is Algiers? I have not been back for nearly thirty years. They would not have me back. I was a young soldier, a para. If I exceeded my duty it was for France. For France. It was my duty to exceed my duty. Sure, we tortured, maimed, killed. But for France. For France.'

I'd wondered who he was, who they'd sent me. Now I knew. They'd sent me a psychopath.

He turned his attention back to me, which wasn't much of a relief. 'Mr Diamond,' he said, savouring my name, clicking his tongue on the final consonant. 'Mr Diamond. The penalty for your crimes is high. Maybe thirty, maybe forty years inside. Or perhaps you would rather we made a deal?'

'What kind of deal?'

'We believe it was Bigman who told us of the gang in the Hotel Majestique.'

'I still think it was Flaherty, despite the voice. Or at least a friend of his. But so what? What's it to do with me?'

'We want Bigman.'

'And? I don't know who he is.'

'You have given us the only tangible evidence we have of him. The only tangible evidence of his existence, much less his identity. For months we have been aware of this shadowy figure, this intellect working behind the operations of the most appalling terrorist groups in Europe. All this time we have suspected: now, perhaps, we know. We know that this man, this Bigman, exists. And you will lead us to him.'

'Look,' I said, in my most reasonable voice. 'I'd like to help. I really would . . .'

The flat black glasses stared back at me. 'Have you ever been to prison?' he asked. 'Have you ever been gang-raped?'

'You've got the wrong man! I can't help! I'd like to! I'd love to! But I can't!'

'Maybe not. But you are all we have got. Think about it.'

'Think about what? Look,' I was back to being reasonable. 'Look, I'll help you all I can. But I can't promise the results. I don't know who Bigman is.'

'We are aware of this. You are a small cog, a tiny cog, in a massive machine. We understand that. We are not unreasonable.' He took the dark glasses off to prove this point, and failed. His eyes were a brown so pale they were almost yellow, and after dark glasses and in the gloomy cell the pupils were huge. 'You are a faint lead, but you are the only lead we have. We know where your Mr Mahon – Mr Flaherty to you – is hiding. We will lead you to him; he will perhaps lead us to Bigman.' He replaced the dark glasses quickly.

'It won't work. You think Bigman wanted Flaherty dead; I think Flaherty wanted me dead. But either way, you're not going to get a chain from me to Bigman.'

'You are the only chance we have.' The dark glasses mocked. 'And we are the only chance you have.'

'Cheers. Have you spoken to Major bar Hilai?'

'There has been no need. Major bar Hilai has returned to her normal duties. This is a French operation now.'

A few days passed. Dracula didn't come back, my meals were regular and so were my bowels, so everything was relatively fine. And then they let me out.

It was night. I was bustled out of my cell by a couple of policemen. They wore capes and the capes were wet. Outside was a car. Chambers was in it already. A policeman in the front held a handgun. It was only aimed in the approximate direction of our bellies, but the threat was quite sufficient. Neither of us spoke.

The rain dotted the windows and smeared the streetlights. We raced through empty streets, with motorcycle escorts front and rear, and I did not dare ask myself where I was going. The end of the journey was a relief. Somewhere in the suburbs the car stopped. I was bundled out; Chambers followed. A bunch of car keys was thrust into my hand. 'You will find the documentation you require inside,' said a policeman. 'Go!'

'Where?'

'I believe you have an address. A Rome address?'

Good grief, I thought. 'Good grief!' I said. 'I'd forgotten that.'

'You have remembered it now?'

'Yes.'

'It is as well. *Bon voyage.* And Mr Thorpe, Mr Diamond. Do not return to France. Ever. Or you will be imprisoned; the Comte de Monte Cristo will have nothing, nothing on you.' He laughed. It was another joke without humour.

I stood blankly in the rain. 'Open the car door then,' said Chambers. Like me his clothes were too light for this weather. His hair was flattened, and the streetlight picked out the flesh between the strands.

'Okay.' I unlocked the door. It gave an efficient German click, and I climbed in. Reaching over, I unfastened Chambers' door and let him in.

'Where to?' he asked.

'Rome.'

'Where are we now?'

I shook my head and started the engine. 'Search me.'

There were better places to search, however. On the shelf in front of him was a collection of maps and documents. One of the maps was of Paris; to the south-east a hand-drawn arrow told us '*Vous êtes ici*'. I banged around for a gear using my unfamiliar right hand, found first at the second attempt, and pulled off. 'Which way?'

'End of the road, turn right. Look out for the level crossing. There's a post box on the left, say eight hundred yards down the street, and if it wasn't dark you'd see a ruined windmill on the right. The rivers here all flow north; we'll be crossing a minor watershed about now, and then . . .'

'Hold it!' I hit the brake and we came to a stop. The pedals were in the same order, but the gear lever was back to front and, momentarily confused, I stalled. 'Shit.'

'What's up. What did we stop for?'

'It was all bull, wasn't it? That business with the map. You didn't really read all that.'

He turned his crafty face to me. 'It's all true,' he said. His voice was more convincing than his face.

'What are you? A rally driver?'

'It's MI7.'

'MI7?'

'MI7,' he confirmed. 'Military Intelligence Cartography Section. We make the maps, old boy. We make the maps.'

I drove most of the night. There was a packet of fags in the glove compartment. 'Thoughtful,' said Chambers. Every so often I stopped, pulling in to the unfamiliar wrong side of the road and having a cigarette and a rest. Once when I stopped I dozed, and Chambers let me sleep.

When I woke a grey band of dawn was lighting the sky. We drove a few more miles. The sun peeped over a wooded hill ahead of us. It wasn't the only thing spying on us. 'Are they still following?'

I checked in the mirror. 'Yep. Any idea who they are?'

'Be optimistic. Assume they're the French security services, checking we're doing as we were told.'

'That's optimistic! I don't know about you but I'm here because they told me I'd face forty years inside if I didn't come.'

He was smiling. 'Mmmm. They would tell you that.'

'Are you trying to tell me something?'

'Mum's the word, old man. Mum's the word.'

We drove on in silence. The Citroen on our tail was replaced by a Renault. My neck ached, my collarbone, though healed, still hurt me. Even the nose Flaherty had thumped was worrying me again. 'I need breakfast.'

'I need a smoke.'

'We'll pull in for some fags if you like. They left me my credit cards. I'll have to buy petrol, I expect.'

'I meant opium.'

'You must have been without for months. Why the sudden craving?'

'Not months, old man.' He held out his left hand for my inspection. It shook in a way that was no reflection on BMW engineering.

'You mean you were getting it in prison?' I asked, incredulous. 'It was all I could do to get food; the only fag I saw in the time we were there was being pressed against the side of my head. Is that how they got you to come along? Bribed you with junk?'

'Nothing like that.' He smiled weakly. 'Do you know how old I am?'

'Fifty?'

'I'm forty-one. I've been an addict for twenty years.'

'And?'

'And I'm stuck with it. I'll do anything, anything at all for a smoke.'

Conversationally, I mentioned that I thought heroin was for injecting, not smoking. 'Result of a cure, old man. I used to mainline.' He pulled up his sleeve. A series of old scars, laced with broken red capillaries, lined his inner arm. 'They gave me a sort of aversion therapy. Hepatitis, AIDS, showed me the lot. Kept sticking needles into me and showing me the pictures. It worked. I can't inject.'

'But you still smoke it.'

'I still need it.'

We pulled off the road. The Renault pulled up behind us. I sat in the car waiting for someone to get out of the Renault, but they seemed to be waiting for us. 'Can't sit here all day,' I said.

'I can.' A bare statement, unembellished by 'old man' or any other dated military slang.

I looked at Chambers. His drawn face was yellow, and the yellow came through the tan like an image seen through water. Dangerous beads of sweat gathered on his harelip. His pale eyes were very sunken, and the pupils were tiny despite the bright daylight. 'Are you all right?' I asked, which is just the sort of bloody stupid thing I would say to a junkie going into cold turkey.

'Ask the chaps behind if they have any smack.'

I was amazed. 'I wouldn't have thought of that,' I admitted. 'Are you sure they won't just lock me up?'

'Any pot in a storm,' he said, and it was only when I was walking to the Renault that I realized it was a joke.

Before I got there the passenger got out. He wore dark glasses. Well he would, wouldn't he? I smiled. 'Avay view any smack?' I asked.

'Eh?'

'Smack, junk, heroin, opium? Le opium?'

A stream of words swept over me like a foreign language broadcast on an unfamiliar wavelength, followed by a single word I caught. *Oui*.

He went back to the car. The driver got out, stretched his neck, and grunted. He was very Germanic, with a thick neck and fair hair cropped short. 'Cocaine?' he asked.

'I'll ask my friend,' I said.

I went back to the BMW and reported to Chambers. His grin was a rictus, but he seemed willing to accept the cocaine. He got out of the BMW and into the back of the Renault. The driver had laid two lines of white powder on a paperback book. With the tube of a ballpoint pen, Chambers sniffed one and then the other, shutting his eyes. I have never moved in cocaine circles. Where I live, a high is a supermarket bag and a tube of glue. The driver offered me the book and the pen but I shook my head. 'Driving,' I said. He shrugged, relaid the lines of white, and sniffed himself.

Chambers and I went back to our car. I still hadn't eaten, but everyone else seemed keen to move on. Chambers was looking far happier. 'Good stuff,' he said. 'Not the same, but good stuff.'

I pulled out. There was a little more traffic on the road than there had been, and the Renault was a couple of trucks behind us now, as I checked in my mirror. 'How did you know they'd have something for you?' I asked suspiciously.

'They're part of the operation, old boy. They were sure to have some.'

This made no sense to me at all. 'I thought they were French police. You said they were.'

'Did I? Must have been a mistake.'

His eyeballs were different now, and his pupils had grown large. I had seen pupils like that before, recently, in a police cell in Paris. 'What's going on?' I asked him.

'You really don't want to know,' he told me.

'I really do.'

'Believe me,' he said, 'you don't.'

He was energetic now, twisting his shoulders and neck all the time to look at things through the window. 'Let me drive,' he told me.

There was a layby ahead. I pulled up; a few trucks thundered by, rocking the BMW. I climbed out and walked round; Chambers squirmed over from seat to seat.

I was out of the car, in the warm noon of a French summer. Thrushes sang. Flies buzzed round a litter bin at the side of the layby. I rubbed my tired face. Whatever was going on – and Chambers obviously knew more about it than me – I didn't like it. The decision to do a runner came quickly, but too late. I'd have done better to have taken the car, and Chambers too if necessary. I'd have travelled faster and got further.

I made a dash along the roadside as the Renault pulled in. Chambers saw me go and wound down the window. 'Hey!'

Chambers wasn't the problem; the Renault was. It had been pulling up behind the BMW, but when the driver saw me running it pulled out again into the traffic, with a squeal and a gaggle of horns, and swerved back into the layby near me. Too near. The passenger got out, threw himself at my feet in a practised rugby tackle, and felled me just like that. I landed heavily on the shattered tarmac, and the wind left me.

They took me back to the BMW. Chambers and my escort spoke rapidly in French, and I wished again I understood more of the language. Chambers was given a gun, and I was told to drive after all. I walked back to the driver's door and Chambers did his squirming again. I sat down without looking at him, started the engine, indicated, waited for a break in the traffic, and pulled smoothly away; I guess it was the effect of the gun, but I felt like someone taking a driving test.

Chambers' high was wearing off now. We travelled in ugly silence. Once I lost the Renault but he told me to slow down until it had caught up with us. It was the only conversation we had until the following day, when we reached Mont Blanc and the border, and in between I had slept in the car, with the men from the Renault in the back and a gun to my head all night. Despite my exhaustion I did not sleep well.

SEVENTEEN

We got through the border without incident. We had newly forged British passports which had been made to look worn with age. I was Joseph King, according to the passport, a teacher by profession; my companion was Charles Henry Saunders, a cartographer. Or perhaps this passport wasn't a forgery. I couldn't be bothered to call him by any other name, however, so Chambers he remained.

He was in a bad way again, but this time he got no sympathy from me. When he asked me to pull up I refused; it was only when he threatened me with the gun that he got what he wanted. Our escort drew up behind us. It was an Alfa Romeo now, an old one, and though the car had changed and the people in it, nothing much else had. Chambers was refuelled on cocaine and we drove on.

The drug made him talkative. To start with, this annoyed me. Three days' driving, with only limited stops and no chance to relax, had gnarled the muscles in my neck to tree roots. My damaged shoulder still ached. I was an automaton with a manual gearbox. But after maybe half an hour of resisting Chambers' chatter I realized I was interested.

'You've got to hand it to Bigman,' he said. 'It's bloody clever.'

'What is?'

'This plan. I wonder when he decided you'd be the fall-guy? He doesn't tell me things like that.' For a moment Chambers was mournful. 'He was my fag, you know, at school, but he doesn't trust me as much as he should.'

I let the fall-guy business pass for the time being. 'You know who Bigman is?'

'Of course, old boy. How do you think I got into this business?

Rupert's been a good friend to me for a long time. He's paid for the junk, you know.'

'And the cures?'

'No, never the cures.' He paused again, lost in happy memories, before repeating himself. 'He's been a good friend to me for a long time.'

'It must be nice to know what's going on,' I said wistfully.

'Oh it is, it is.'

Neither of us spoke for a while. I concentrated on how to frame my next question and got too close to a truck ahead. 'Steady, old man,' said Chambers.

'Sorry. You were telling me all you know.'

'Was I? Oh yes.' God bless talkative cocaine. 'Where was I?'

I didn't know how long this mood was going to last. What did I need to know most? 'You were talking about what was going to happen to me,' I said.

'Rupert's clever. He doesn't tell me what he's thinking – we haven't met in years – but I know him. I know how his mind works. You're being set up, old boy.'

'Set up for what?'

'Rupert's getting out of this game. He only got into it by accident. The CIA approached him, as Chairman of the Croupier Group. Croupier have a lot of dealings in the Middle East and Rupert knows General Tassat. The Americans wanted their hostages out of Qafadya, and used him to negotiate a deal. They'd supply Qafadya with arms if Qafadya freed the hostages.'

'The Americans bombed Qafadya,' I reminded him. 'Did the deal go wrong?'

'Don't know, old boy,' he said blandly. 'Anyway, Rupert met a few bigwigs in Qafadya and found out about the Cairo Accord, and he also knew a few people in the Mafia. You a Freemason, old chap?'

'Yes,' I lied, to keep him talking.

'I expect that's why you're involved, eh? Anyway, Rupert's Mafia friends were looking for a new way of distributing drugs, and

Rupert, I imagine, decided that if the drugs were distributed on the Cairo Accord network it would be almost impossible to trace the source. So that's what he set up. That book you were carrying is full of information. Three lines up from the bottom of each page, second column in, is a map reference; fifth line down, third column, and with the first and last digits removed, is a telephone number. The courier goes to the map reference, finds a payphone, makes a local call, and the chap at the other end knows the goods are ready; this chap then gives a page and column number from the same book. There's a map reference at the top of the specified column and that's where the drop should take place, and beneath it is the day of the month and the time. It's brilliant.'

It was certainly ingenious, and though it seemed a little compli-cated to me, I've no doubt it was a lot less cumbersome than many rival arrangements. 'But Rupert's getting out?' I asked.

'Flaherty seems to have let him down somehow. And I think the Israeli tart worries him. I don't know; I only know what I learned in Paris.'

I had forgotten Rebecca's role in all this; it was something else to leave to one side for the time being. 'Are the French in on this officially?'

'Come off it, old chap. But junk's the word worldwide.' He mused and then smiled. 'The man who gave you a pasting was one of us. Did you see his eyes? A true user. Don't know how he keeps down his job.'

'I expect he's good at it,' I said from experience. 'What do we do when we get to Rome?'

'That's simple. Flaherty knows you. He knows you're an ama-teur, out of your depth. He won't be expecting you to kill him.'

'I won't kill him,' I said.

'You will. You see, Flaherty's boys have visited your father. He's dead, old chap; your father's dead.'

I sat blankly behind the wheel, and for a second time Chambers had to urge caution as I got too close to the traffic ahead. Da was dead. Da.

I didn't know what to do.

I never bloody do.

Chambers chattered on blithely. 'Anyway, you're going to kill Flaherty, then evidence is going to be planted that you're Bigman.'

'Me!'

'Why not? The police need someone for their files. Bigman's retiring – I think, honestly, Rupert found it all a bit too risky and a bit too sordid – and you, by chance, have been to the right places and have met the right people. Well, enough of them anyway. You're the perfect fall-guy.'

There was too much to think about here. 'Tell me about MI7,' I said, playing for time while I thought.

'My father is a professor of geography, you know. I've always been good with maps. When I left Cambridge I was enrolled in MI7. They didn't know about my drugs problem then, of course! And I was shipped out to Greece because of my Greek mother. I've worked in Greece, Turkey, the whole eastern Med from Yugoslavia right round to Qafadya.'

'Doing what?' I was still turning other matters over in my mind; my curiosity about Chambers' sordid career was superficial.

'Plotting the installations that aren't on the commercial maps. I'm good at it.' There was no pride here; this was a statement of fact and I believed him. 'That's why they turn a blind eye to my little problem.'

His speech was losing its brightness now; the drug was wearing off.

He slept soon after. Da was dead; Bigman was the chairman of a major British company; I was to be set up. It was too much to think about – I needed to act. At the next filling station I bought myself a pair of dark glasses along with the petrol. It seemed somehow significant; it was the first step down the road to action.

Perhaps it was the lack of sleep. There was an intensity to my thoughts I had never known before, a singleness of purpose. Without realizing it I had changed a great deal since that day Flaherty had come to call and Mulligan's head had disintegrated on my threadbare rug. I sat behind my dark glasses and glared defiance at the world.

Chambers was still asleep. I wondered about taking the gun from his hand but dismissed the idea. I no longer felt like going home. Da was dead and I wanted to see this through. I drove on through the day with the Alfa always behind and slept at gunpoint that night. There was probably a landscape around me. It was probably beautiful. Mont Blanc must have been beautiful, and the summer sun must have caught the snows and made the mountains into gems and jewels beyond price. But there was no room for beauty in my mind, no room for the sun, and all I remember clearly about that journey was a burning factory we passed on the road to Rome. The fire had been burning for some time. The windows were full of flame and the walls above the windows were stained with a shock of smoke. We slowed almost to a stop as we gawped, and the ambulances fetched out the dead. Then the traffic was accelerating. I looked in the mirror. Smoke fingered the sky; it lingered in our hair.

All roads lead to Rome, including mine. I had circled the Mediterranean to get here and spiralled my way in like an eagle before a kill. Or at least, I hoped that's how it would be. I had an address, Ria Mazzanati 287. Flaherty would be there. That was all I needed.

Rome's streets were high and flaking. They were trenches cut through like archaeological digs, containing the past. The buildings had regular windows and irregular walls, and the peeling shutters were open like arms that expect an embrace. Beneath the cracked walls and the shutters were shops. These were dark and mysterious, hung with peppers and onions. Churches stood, broad-shouldered and proud, flexing their muscles against the crush of housing and commerce. They were dark inside too, and peppered with candles, and theirs was a different mystery.

There was another map among our papers; Rome spread out like a web, and Chambers found our destination quickly. He told me not to drive straight to the house, but to stop at the end of the road. The Alfa had gone, but when I drew up a Fiat halted behind me. 'What do I kill him with?' I asked.

'They'll have the weapon,' said Chambers. He was not really interested in what was going on. He was waiting for his next fix. But 'they' had got out of their Fiat. They stood by the doors of the BMW, waiting for me, and studying the street through dark glasses. I opened the door, stood, and stretched; they handed me a short-nosed pistol. 'Safety catch up,' said the man by my door. 'Down to fire. Have it down in your pocket please. It is better you should blow your own foot off than fail to kill your enemy, yes?'

His accent was Italian. His surname, at a guess, was Borgia.

I set off down the street. The gun was bulky in the pocket of my sports jacket and my finger kept straying towards the trigger.

It was a long walk to 287. I had the impression of people avoiding me, as though my dark glasses told them what I had in mind. I counted off the house numbers as I walked, losing the sequence sometimes at shops but then recovering it. I slowed as I approached the upper two hundreds; time slowed down too. At 287 I stopped, knocked on the door, and let myself in. A flight of stairs led me directly from the street to the upper apartments. I climbed it slowly. There were scuff marks on the wall, and a single door at the first landing. I thought of the safe house in Camden, but I felt no sympathy for Flaherty who spent his days scuttling from one such place to the next with one eye always over his shoulder.

Again I knocked and tried the door, but this time it was locked. I waited. There was a peephole. I sensed an eye looking out, and heard bolts drawn. 'Jack Diamond?'

The door opened. I looked at him. 'Flaherty.'

'To be sure and I thought you'd be in prison by now. What the fuck happened in Paris?' If he had seen the gun in my hand he was ignoring it.

'I left before the siege began,' I lied. I don't know why I lied. I don't know why I didn't shoot him the moment he opened the door, as had been my intention. 'Tell me about my dad.'

'Your dad?' Flaherty, fugitive, was looking old. His shoulders looked as if they'd collapsed round his chest; his clothes seemed ill-fitting and awkward. 'You've heard then,' he said.

'I've heard.'

He acknowledged the gun with his eyes now. 'I see.' There was a long pause. 'You'd better come in. He was a good man.'

I stepped inside and carefully shut the door behind me without taking my eyes off Flaherty. He was looking still older now, but he was not looking scared.

'We'll miss the funeral,' he said. 'I'm sorry.'

'Sorry!' I raised the gun. Incredulity made me mad. 'Sorry! And what did he die for? It would have been bad enough he'd died for the Republic! God knows that would have been bad enough! But to have died for you and your crooked bloody deals with some crooked bloody English nobleman!'

Flaherty's voice was gentle. 'There's no reason to any death, Jack.'

'I bloody well know that!' I tried to pull the trigger. 'But you were the one who gave the orders.'

'I'm sorry about your dad. I'm not asking for mercy. But understand me. I am truly sorry about his death.'

'I'll never understand you,' I said, but the moment for shooting had passed.

Anything I might have added – and I don't know what it might have been – was interrupted by a knock at the door. I turned and opened it mechanically. I don't know who I'd expected to see. I certainly hadn't expected Rebecca.

'Hello, Jack,' she said.

She came in. In her hands she carried a book. I recognized it. *Advanced Mathematical Tables*. 'Hello,' I said.

She looked past me, or was it through me, and spoke to Flaherty. 'I was wanting a word with Mr Mahon.'

'Hello there,' said Flaherty. 'I don't think we've met.' He was glad of the interruption. 'Jack, introduce us.'

'This is Mr Flaherty' – I realized I had never known his first name – 'of the Derry Brigade of the Irish National Liberation Army; this is Major bar Hilai of the Shin Beth, the Israeli internal security service.'

'Currently I am seconded,' she said, 'to Mossad. We are working on a case of international importance.' Like mine and Flaherty's, her voice carried no emotion. We were like nervous actors at a first read-through, saying the lines as we got to them but not managing the intonation yet.

'I'm pleased to meet you,' he said. 'Come in. Would you like some wine?'

He led us through into a kitchen. There was a formica-topped table and four chairs upholstered in plastic. From a free-standing refrigerator Flaherty pulled out a bottle of white wine; he got the glasses from the draining board. 'Say when.'

'That's enough, thank you,' she replied.

'And you, Jack?'

I said nothing but he poured me a glass anyway. 'Your very good health,' he offered. We raised our glasses dutifully, though it was hardly an appropriate toast. 'And now,' he said, 'what can I do for you?'

'This book,' she replied, laying it on the table.

'And where did you get it, if I may ask?'

'Mr Diamond would have left it in the desert. I thought it better to look after it.'

'Careless, Jack.' Flaherty shook his heavy head, as if after killing my da he was taking on parental responsibility. 'Very careless.'

'Anyway,' continued Rebecca, 'our experts have looked at it. It's obviously not a genuine series of mathematical tables; the numbers make no sense. We need to know what it is. A code book?'

'I'll tell you about it later,' he said. 'When you've got me safe in a police station. How did you find me, by the way?'

'Mr Diamond is an amateur. He gave me this address. We have been watching it for several days. I assume you were always intending to be here yourself to receive the book?'

'I was indeed. There's some useful information in that book, to be sure.'

'Such as?'

He smiled. 'The largest drugs and guns ring in Europe, ready for the picking off, or advantage, of anyone who holds the key.' The smile broadened. 'Of course, in return for that key I would expect certain promises.'

'Such as?'

'My freedom. A new identity. Money.'

'That can be arranged.'

I interrupted. 'He killed my da, my father!'

Rebecca turned to me, startled.

'Not personally,' Flaherty hastened to assure her.

'You gave the orders,' I told him.

'Is that why you've got that gun in your hand?' Rebecca asked, still looking at me.

'I came here to kill him.'

'And didn't.'

'Couldn't.'

'You'd better give me the gun.'

Flaherty looked satisfied with these arrangements; Rebecca took the pistol, checked the safety catch, and shot him neatly in the head.

The sound of the bullet was loud in the confined kitchen. Flaherty jerked back in his chair. His eyes were open. There was a third eye in the middle of his forehead. He stared at the ceiling with all three.

Rebecca slowly lowered the gun. Blue smoke licked and curled around us. 'The gun is yours, I believe,' she said.

I stood without taking the gun. I looked at Flaherty, looked across at Rebecca; she met my eye. 'Pour me another drink, please.'

I shook my head, not at her request but at her nerve. 'Is that all you can think of to say?' I marvelled.

In reply she held out her hand. It shook. 'Jack, I am not a natural killer,' she said.

'So why?'

'Someone had to. You wouldn't. I did it for you.'

'What about your mission? Dead he can't give you information?'

'He killed your father,' she repeated, stubbornly.

I didn't have an answer to that so I took her hand, still outstretched, and led her from the kitchen to the adjoining room. Flaherty's corpse sat rigid at the head of the table. *'Pax vobiscum,'* I said softly. 'I'll pray for your depraved Irish soul.'

The next room was a bedroom. 'Why did you do that?' asked Rebecca. 'Why did you say you would pray for him?'

'It's what we do for the dead. Say a prayer, light a candle, have a drink. And maybe another drink.' I drew the curtains. 'And draw the curtains,' I added.

She looked at me seriously, went back into the kitchen, and fetched Flaherty's wine. 'The drink,' she announced. She lifted the bottle. 'To Flaherty,' she said. 'To his death.'

'That's not quite how we do it,' I said, sitting on the bed, 'but I don't suppose it matters.'

She took an unhealthy swig and passed me on the bottle. 'Do you know what I do for a living?' she asked, changing the subject defiantly. There was a dangerous edge to her voice.

'You're a spy.'

'Apart from that?'

I looked at my shoes. 'I'd heard a rumour,' I said.

'I'm what's called a glamour model,' she said. 'I open my legs for cameras.'

'I know.'

'Have you seen my work? I'm good at it. I do it well. I'm good at it.'

'Steady,' I said, for she was close to tears.

'I hate it.'

She fixed me with her eyes and unfastened the buttons of her blouse. She wore nothing beneath. Her familiar unknown breasts were tan and darker, shade and nipple. The shirt fell to the floor and she kicked off her shoes. Her eyes were still fixed on my face;

she was the stripper but I was the one most exposed. She unzipped her jeans, rolled them down with her panties, and stood quite naked before me. 'The rest of the world has seen this,' she said.

'Does that matter?' I asked.

'It means I've no secrets to give as a gift,' she said. And then: 'Doesn't it matter to you?'

Again I had no answer; again I held out my hand. She took it in hers and let me pull her on to the bed. The nylon spread was cheap, cool and slippery. Our lips touched. Our mouths explored.

She rolled on top of me, hitching herself up and kneeling each side of my thighs. Her arms pinned mine. 'Lie still,' she instructed. She took up her hands to open my flies: my cock popped out like a cuckoo when its hour has come. Now she was bending double, stretching her tongue towards the pointed pink cap; she licked round the sensitive edges and along the blue vein on top; she put her tongue to the opening at the end and enfolded it in her hungry lips. Her mouth moved over me deliciously. I was eaten alive and I loved it, but if she wasn't careful I'd be done too soon. So I pushed up with my arms, took her mouth from my cock and kissed her moist lips. 'Cheat,' she told me as I rolled her over. I was in charge now. I kicked off my clothes and was naked above her, stroking the mouth of her vulva with the tip of my prick. 'Tease,' she said. I ducked my mouth to her breasts, pulling at the tip of her proud nipples with my lips, massaging them with my hands, till I ducked myself down. A band of light came between the curtains and lay across her belly. I kissed lower and lower, through the band of light, into the darker hair beneath, until my exploring tongue found her clitoris, her love button. 'No,' she said, and then 'Yes.'

There was the sharp taste of woman there, a sea-breeze tang, a damp beauty. She came with shivers of breath, holding my head to her and then holding me away. 'No more.' And then she was on top of me again, lowering herself over my full penis, lowering and moving herself until everything I had was compressed there inside her and about to burst out. I pulled her over before it was too late. I was on top again, feeling the full length of me sliding in and out of her. Her nails were pain in my back. I pushed my arms straight, so our heads were far apart, and looked down on the body below me, the tight breasts combed to budded nipples, the flat belly, and the dark hair beneath where I could see myself entering and not quite leaving her. The rhythm intensified, a bolero for two, a tango. Our muscles tensed and released. She pushed towards me as I towards her. The tango was louder in our ears. Cadenza, coda, climax. Her back arched. There was that moment of release from my prick, that instant of power and of peace. Then I was done as was she, we were together on the bed, and Flaherty was in his kitchen.

Still linked in our dampness, we held one another. Later we kissed, hugged tightly, and she ran her finger down the scar on my neck; later still we got dressed.

We walked back through the kitchen. A fly had found Flaherty. It ran on busy legs around his wound. I waved a hand to shift it, but it settled again at once.

Rebecca picked up the gun. We walked down the stairs and into the street. 'Which way are you going?' she asked.

'I left Chambers in the car at the end of the road.'

'Is Chambers still with you? I didn't think he'd want to get so involved.'

This reminded me. 'There's a lot I must explain,' I began, but she was looking over my shoulder.

Several police cars were squeezing up the narrow street. Each was topped with a chain of red light that flashed into the shadows and bounced off the walls. 'Perhaps someone heard the shot,' she said. 'I must go.'

Unsure whether I wanted to stop her or not, I let her.

'Contact me at Petroland SA, Via Camino Z,' she said. 'It's a front organization.' Her voice was urgent; the police cars were almost upon us. She turned up the street. 'Goodbye.' And still neither of us spoke of love.

The police cars stopped outside 287. For a moment I thought

I might be inconspicuous enough to slip away, but then Chambers, climbing from the back of the second car, saw me. 'There he is!' he shouted. There was nothing else to do. I put up my hands and let them take me away.

They bustled me, handcuffed, into the back of the same car as Chambers. He wore no handcuffs. I looked at him balefully. The role of privileged informer seemed to suit him, somehow. 'Sorry, old man,' he said, 'but I did say you'd be fingered for Flaherty's murder. Actually you could have got away with it, you know. We're in Vatican City here and the carabinieri had to make all kinds of fuss to come in and get you. That's why we're so late. I expected you'd have got clean away by now. What have you been doing, waiting for us?'

I had nothing to say in return. I looked out of the window at Rome flitting by. I saw fountains and vistas made familiar by films. It seemed a long time since I'd told Flaherty I didn't want to end my days in an Italian jail; many things had changed since then but that ambition hadn't.

Chambers must have read my mind. 'Don't worry,' he said. 'Accidents happen in police cells all the time. We wouldn't want you to live to stand trial now, would we?'

I sat back in the plastic seat and my life lurched from bad to worse.

EIGHTEEN

I was taken to the police station and searched. The carabinieri were somewhat disconcerted not to find a gun on me; they hadn't found one at the scene of the crime either, and they were looking hard. What they did find, however, were some credit cards in the name of someone called Jack Diamond, and among the plastic, forgotten even by me, was a calling card. 'Toole, Joy Associates, Radical Law'. I was allowed one phone call. I didn't want to involve Rebecca, and had no one else to phone, so I phoned Joy.

He was surprisingly helpful and efficient. Within three hours he had an Italian lawyer in there, a good-looking young man with a mind as sharp as his suit. The evidence against me was circumstantial. My fingerprints had been found on a glass in the bedroom, but I wasn't denying I'd been there: if they'd tested, they would probably have found my semen in the sheets, and God knows what they'd have made of that. But there was no weapon, and Flaherty had been dead nearly an hour before I was picked up.

'Your story is simple,' said my lawyer when we had a moment of privacy. 'You and another friend had a drink with the victim earlier in the day. He was a compatriot, and Irishmen abroad are well-known for their clannishness. You then left. You were just returning to his apartment when you were picked up by the police. It is far more credible than the alternative, postulated by the witness Saunders. Indeed, it is far more credible than Saunders: he made his statement and disappeared; the police are looking for him now.'

Italian police cells are no worse than English or French ones, and a good deal warmer. I mooched about, learning some words of Italian from my cell mate. Unfortunately he was a Calabrian;

his accent was as thick as the Irishman in a joke and when I tried out the words I had learned on the guards they thought I was still speaking English.

Five days passed before I even had a hearing. Evidence was presented; bail was requested. My lawyer had already cautioned me against expecting the latter, but the prosecuting magistrate was surprisingly benign and accepted that the evidence against me was inconclusive. They took away my false passport and set bail at thirty million lire. I would have been overjoyed, had I known anyone with thirty million lire. But my luck was turning. 'A woman' – the policeman sketched an hourglass with his hands – 'she came and guaranteed your bail in cash.' It wasn't hard to guess who that woman might be.

I was released into my lawyer's custody that afternoon. 'Who's paying you?' I asked, as Angelo bought me lunch.

'Mr Joy.'

'And who's paying him, I wonder? It was Flaherty himself who said radical lawyers weren't cheap.'

'There are certain organizations. Your defence is being paid for by the Percy Bysshe Shelley Trust, which was established to defend political radicals from imprisonment.'

'They'll have their work cut out! In England today you're considered a radical if you have pink pages in your Filofax. But where does this Shelley Trust raise the money? Royalties on the poems?'

'Hardly. Actually, you'd be surprised how many big businesses take an interest.'

'You're right. I would be surprised. Why should big business be interested in helping political extremists? It's not like it was in the sixties, when everyone was a radical; in Thatcher's Britain radicalism carries about as much political clout as the Flat Earth Society.'

He smiled. 'Numbers are not everything, however. The Angry Brigade was a tiny cell that did great damage; the Red Brigades here in Italy, or the Red Army Faction in West Germany, were equally small. A small contribution towards a cause like the Shelley

Trust, taken from pre-tax profits, may ensure that the company's personnel and property do not become targets. One of your benefactors arrived in Rome recently, as it happens.'

'Really,' I said. 'I must thank him. Who is he?'

'Lord Rupert Pellon of the Croupier Group.'

My interest was suddenly more than sarcastic. 'Lord Pellon?' I tried to hide my eagerness. 'How do you know?'

'I read the financial pages,' he said, and coughed apologetically. 'These days even a Communist has shares.'

'And where's he staying in Rome?'

'How should I know?' he asked, and then looked up. 'Actually, I do know: I saw an article about his apartment in a magazine; he's got a penthouse in a palace.'

A penthouse in a palace! I wondered if he had a sunken bath in his Rolls and a Monet in the stables. There was no question I was out of my depth. But I'd been out of my depth from the start, and you're just as dead in a foot of water as forty fathoms. I wanted to meet Lord Pellon. 'Whereabouts?' I asked as casually as I could.

'I couldn't tell you, but the palace is the headquarters of Croupier Italia SA. I expect it'll be in the phone book.'

After we had eaten Angelo offered to show me his city, but I had other things in mind. 'I'm sure you're busy,' I said.

He shrugged. 'Nothing important.'

'I know you must be,' I insisted. 'If you could just lend me a few thousand lire I'll find my own way round. I'll be fine.'

'You will not see much for a few thousand lire,' he warned.

'I'll be all right.'

He shrugged again. 'Very well. We shall meet tonight at this restaurant. On the Estrolti. At eight o'clock.'

'That would be nice,' I said warmly, and I meant it. Angelo was a nice guy. I'd almost forgotten there were any left. But 'would' is the conditional tense – had you forgotten I had a degree? – and I had my doubts about the conditions for this meeting being fulfilled.

I saw him safely back to his car and then hailed a taxi. 'Via

Camino,' I said. I wanted a talk with Rebecca before seeing Pellon. Rebecca was the only ally left.

We drove round the tatty ruins of the Forum and past a giant cinema organ caked in icing that's called the Victor Emmanuel monument. The Via Camino was in the modern, commercial part of the city. A plaque outside number 7 announced the Italian office of 'Petroland SA (Regd 1984)'. I walked in, and a young lady in an efficient suit raised an eyebrow at me. '*Si?*'

'Rebecca bar Hilai please.'

The woman looked a little concerned but pressed a button on her console and lifted a handset. A conversation followed, in a language I didn't recognize. It certainly wasn't Italian; perhaps it was Hebrew. She put her hand over the receiver. 'Your name?' she asked me.

'Jack Diamond.'

There was another stream of words, with my name garbled into it, and then she put the handset down. 'Miss bar Hilai does not work from this office,' she told me, which figured because this commercial respectability was hardly the natural backdrop for glamour photography. 'But Mr Constein is familiar with her work. If you will wait he will see you in a moment.' I hoped it was only her undercover work Mr Constein was familiar with; I was not in the mood for a discussion of the finer points of her buttocks.

I sat uncomfortably in a low chair that was all tubular steel and suspended leather, turning the pages of a fancy Italian magazine. I did not have a long wait. 'Mr Diamond?'

Mr Constein was very tall and dignified in an elegant grey silk suit. We shook hands. 'How can I help you? he enquired of the air two inches over my head. He looked vaguely familiar and I realized he was the man who had met Rebecca off the Algiers plane.

'Rebecca, Miss bar Hilai, told me to find her here. Look, I've a lot to tell her. Can you get a message to her, arrange a meeting?'

'Come to my office.'

I followed him into a lift. It was a posh lift. Even the walls were carpeted. It was like travelling by padded cell. We climbed a few floors and were released.

His room was at the end of a corridor. It was large and well furnished, with a desk providing the focus at one end and a coffee table at the other. 'Sit down,' he offered. 'Make yourself comfortable.' There was a chair opposite the desk but I chose the settee by the table. Behind me the windows gave a view of the geometric offices opposite; to break up the geometry Mr Constein had a vast cheese plant in a planter. 'My fiancée has spoken of you,' he said.

'Fiancée?'

He sat down and offered me a cigarette from an onyx box. 'In our business personal attachments make one vulnerable, so we keep our engagement secret. When our present term of duty is complete, however, we shall marry.'

'Oh.' I was a bit stymied here so I took a cigarette, even though I'd not had one for days and thought I had given up. 'Er. I was hoping to see her.'

'I am perfectly capable of taking any message you wish to give her,' he said, offering me a light. But there was one message I wanted to give her that he would never pass on.

'I know who Bigman is,' I said.

'Bigman?' The name apparently meant nothing to him; I suddenly realized it would mean nothing to Rebecca either.

'Bigman,' I repeated. 'He's behind the Cairo Accord.'

Constein sat back, crossed his legs, and pressed his elegant fingers together. 'Go on.'

I told him what I knew and what I'd put together. 'The Cairo Accord was formed to give the terrorist groups more leverage in the arms market. It centres round Qafadya; the Qafadyan government is the only government that openly acknowledges its membership of the Accord. Last year Lord Pellon, the British businessman, was secretly invited by the CIA to negotiate on their behalf for the release of the American hostages in Qafadya. His negotiations apparently failed – maybe the Irangate affair scared the CIA off – but along the way Lord Pellon found out about the Cairo Accord, and recognized its potential.

'It seems he already had Mafia friends: I don't know the details but I'd investigate Freemasonry if I were you. Anyway, Pellon's plan was that drugs should be distributed through the same network used for arms smuggling, and he devised a code using a book called *Advanced Mathematical Tables* which informed those in the know of where and when drops would be made. But recently, alarmed by one or two things, he has decided to pull out. The French police are after him, certainly, and maybe everyone else too, but you are the first person in a position to do anything about him to be told his identity.'

He continued to look at his steepling hands. 'Go on.'

'That's it,' I said. There didn't seem to be much left of my cigarette. I put it out, wondering why I'd bothered smoking it at all.

'That's it?' He was politely surprised. 'You have no evidence?'

'Investigate,' I told him. 'The evidence will turn up.'

He smiled at his fingers. 'Mr Diamond. You over-estimate me and my organization. I am in no position to investigate Lord Pellon. And frankly, even if I were, I should want more than your cock and bull story to go on. Lord Pellon is one of the richest men in Europe. Why should he be interested in terrorism? Or drug-running?'

'I don't know. I'm just passing on what I've been told.'

'And you are a very credulous man. I, fortunately, am less credulous. Rebecca told me you were an amateur. She seems to find something engaging about your incompetence; I find nothing of the sort. I cannot claim to like you, Mr Diamond. I have heard what you have to say, and shall file it appropriately. But I cannot act on it, nor recommend action. No action is required.' He gave me a formal smile. 'Goodbye.'

There wasn't much point in prolonging the interview: all I could think of adding was that his fiancée was a damn good lay, but I'd already been beaten up enough. I wondered if he'd guessed that

Rebecca and I had slept together and decided he probably had. It would explain his coldness. 'Goodbye,' I said, formal in return.

'You can see yourself out.' It was not a question.

I returned to the lift, and from there to reception. I walked out into the street and looked for a taxi, but there weren't any to be seen.

'Major Diamond!' said a voice I knew.

I turned round. 'Major Fahd! What are you doing in Rome?'

'The same as you, I imagine, Major Diamond.' He insisted on the spurious rank. 'I am here for the conference. Have you been visiting Colonel Constein?' He cocked his head at the Israeli building. 'I was on my way to pay my compliments myself.'

'Really?'

'A delightful man to do business with, I find.'

I muttered something ambiguous.

'Where are you going now?'

'Er. Nowhere special.'

'You have a car?'

'I'll get a taxi.'

'Perhaps. But cabs in Rome are not so easy to find. I shall be proud to give you a lift.'

I wondered why he was being so nice, but could hardly turn him down without good reason. 'That's very good of you.'

'Excellent,' said Fahd. 'I shall only be a moment, then we shall travel together. I gather you were of assistance to our embassy in Algeria.' That explained his friendliness: perhaps the Qafadyans were going to give me a medal?

He led me back to his car. It was parked, conveniently and illegally, across the pavement. In Italy they think bumpers are for bumping, which is reasonable, but despite the ubiquitous dents Fahd's car was beautiful, a two-door Mercedes, and he opened it for me with evident pride. I moved a pile of documents that concealed a heavy gun and sat inside. 'You would like music while you wait, perhaps?' he said. 'I have CD.' He pressed a button but nothing happened. 'Of course,' he muttered, fitting the ignition key and giving it a half turn. I recognized the record. Everyone recognizes it. Fleetwood Mac. Bloody *Rumours*.

'Thanks,' I said.

'My pleasure. I shall not be long. I shall see you soon.'

I sincerely hope not, I thought. I watched him go into the office, then I shifted the papers again and climbed over to the driver's seat. The gun, an Israeli pistol, a Desert Eagle, was snub-nosed and smug at my side.

NINETEEN

I stopped the music. I'd had enough rumours: I needed a certainty. I also needed a telephone book. Phone boxes in Rome are about as conspicuous as Ian Paisley's compassion but at last I found one. I guess the Italian telephone service hasn't been privatized because not only did the telephone work but there was even a phone book. The Croupier Group was listed. I made a note of the address, Palazzi Cavalcanti, on the back of one of Fahd's papers and drove off.

The next thing I needed was a street map; I picked one up outside Mussolini's surprisingly modern-looking railway station, and wondered if the trains still ran on time. And finally I needed a church. This one was easy.

Despite being squashed into a row of terraces and shops the church was broad and handsome. The inside was free of the noise and smells of Rome. Rome was squawking birdsong, car horns and the rumble of engines, the fragrance of pizza and urine, the fragments of transistorized music and the popgun squeals of scooters; inside was quiet, and dark, and the air was dyed with incense.

I knelt before the altar. I couldn't confess, didn't know what I should say to a priest. I didn't know what I should say to God either, but a few words seemed in order. 'Hello, God,' I began. It wasn't how I'd been taught to pray but this wasn't how I'd been taught to live. 'I won't keep You long. I'd just like to put in a word for my da . . .'

It was getting late. I went back to the car. A million starlings plagued the dusky sky or perched on the cracked sills of the buildings, where they stained the stucco with black and white streaks that unfurled like tattered flags from the windows. I cruised through a strange area, a little like Belgravia, magnificence and tattiness side by side, and found the Palazzi Cavalcanti, large and Palladian, with a broad portico of handsome columns surrounded by graceful stone steps. The palace was distinguished from its neighbours by its better condition and a sign on the door that said 'The Croupier Group of Companies Roma Italia'. I climbed the stairs, feeling like a Medici, and walked in.

'Is Lord Pellon at home?' I asked airily.

The smart receptionist looked up at me critically. 'You have an appointment?' I'd met her sister. She worked for Constein.

'Not exactly. Just tell him Mr Diamond would like to see him.'

'Mr Diamond?'

'Correct.'

'I cannot disturb Lord Pellon.'

I sat down without being asked. 'Yes, you can,' I told her. The nose of the revolver I'd found in Fahd's glove compartment pushed aggressively over the edge of my jacket pocket.

I didn't see her press the alarm, but the room was suddenly full of security men. They wore ochre uniforms and – fancy that – sunglasses. Fahd's gun was still in my pocket, still pointing at the receptionist. I didn't bother to stand. I didn't need to.

'Put down your weapon!' demanded a guard.

'Not until I see Lord Pellon.'

'You will be shot.'

'So will the girl.'

The leader of the guards summoned a minion, and there was a consultation. I sat in the firing line of half a dozen machine pistols and fingered Fahd's gun. I should have been anxious, or afraid, or guilty about holding this woman at gunpoint, but something had happened to my nerves; all the ganglia had seized up and I felt neither hope nor fear. The consultation ended.

'What's the decision?' I asked.

'We want you to put down the gun.'

They were consistent at least, which made a change, but I shook my head. 'Not until I've spoken to Lord Pellon,' I repeated.

A light flashed on the desk. The receptionist moved to answer it, looked at me, and moved back. 'Go ahead,' I told her.

She picked up the receiver, still looking at me, still looking terrified. 'It is his lordship,' she muttered.

'Good,' I said. 'You can tell him I'm here.'

She listened to whatever he had to say, afraid of interrupting him, afraid of annoying me, and then cleared her throat. 'Lord Pellon? There's a disturbance here. A man wants to see you.'

Pellon prattled something electrical.

'He has a gun,' she told him.

The electrical noises got louder. 'Diamond,' she said, in reply to an unheard question. There was a silence at the end of the phone, and then a concise babble. 'He will see you,' she said. 'But you must be unarmed.'

'No good.'

She didn't need to pass this on; he obviously heard. Then the telephone went dead. She stared at the receiver and then at me. 'He is gone.'

'He'll be back,' I assured her, taking the receiver and putting it back on its cradle.

We waited and he was, arriving through the double doors at the end of the hall. I had seen press photographs, I suppose, but he was taller than I had expected, and tougher. 'Mr Diamond?' His voice was controlling and controlled. The guards relaxed.

I stood up. 'Correct. Lord Pellon?'

'At your service.'

'You've heard of me?' I asked. I wanted to make sure he knew who he was talking to.

'We have mutual friends.' He waved the guards to lower their guns. 'Would you like to step this way?'

He was brave enough. He knew I was armed but he did not allow this to disturb him. We entered a lift. Constein's lift had been a padded cell; this was a mobile art gallery, spotlit paintings and bugger-all furniture. The lift climbed silently, as we stood side by side. He was much my height and build.

The penthouse, out of character for this venerable building, seemed tastefully austere and entirely in character for Lord Pellon. It must have been added to the original structure, because Palladio didn't go in much for full-length plate-glass picture windows and split-level conference areas with concealed lighting. A couple of ochre-uniformed guards were standing at the door when we arrived, but Pellon signalled them to go into the lift. I watched the lights above the lift door that told me they were going down, and was not deceived: they were never far away.

'Would you like a drink, Mr Diamond?' he asked. His accent was similar to Chambers', but without the hopeful, hopeless bonhomie. 'I've just bought rather a good whisky and I've been meaning to try it.' He'd probably bought the distillery. I followed him to a cocktail bar that would have graced the QE2 and he fetched a bottle. 'Thirty-five-year-old malt. Only a few years younger than me – or you.' The glasses were ready on a tray. 'Sit down.'

I already had, choosing a seat that left my back to the wall and my face to the lift. But my back has long been to the wall and it's too late for a facelift. 'It's time we met,' I told him.

'Really?' he asked. 'Why, pray? By the way, I think you can put the gun down now.'

For the first time I had a chance to look at him properly. He was right, he was about my age, which made sense if he had been at school with Chambers, but his groomed hair was as grey as his suit and made him seem older and more responsible. He handed me a glass. I did what he wanted and laid the gun on the table. The Desert Eagle symbol on the gun made the weapon look like a toy.

'You're Bigman,' I told him.

He looked at me quizzically, running a hand over the crinkled ridges of his hair. 'Yes?' If he had been of a different class he'd have added 'So what?'

'You're Bigman, for Christ's sake. You co-ordinate killers, push drugs, and God only knows what besides.'

'And?'

His urbanity was shocking. 'And nothing. Isn't it enough that you're doing all this?'

'I take it dear old Bendy has been talking,' he said by way of a reply.

'Bendy?'

'You probably know him as Saunders, or perhaps Chambers, but to me he'll always be dear old Bendy. I fagged for him at school, you know. He always talked too much.'

'The only secret a junkie can keep is his habit,' I said. It didn't mean much though it sounded good. But I felt a surprising loyalty to Chambers, to Bendy. 'He isn't the only one who's spoken to me by any means.'

Pellon sipped his whisky, licked his upper lip, and smiled encouragingly. 'Tell me what you know. I'll correct any details you get wrong.'

'You are a very rich and important man. The CIA used you to negotiate the release of certain American hostages from Qafadya.'

'My companies have strong connections in Qafadya, as it happens,' he agreed. 'General Tassat is a friend.'

'During the course of these negotiations you learned of an agreement between a large number of left-wing and terrorist organizations, called the Cairo Accord.'

'Not quite. The Cairo agreement was signed after my involvement began, though the organization was already established.'

I acknowledged the correction. 'You saw that this illicit network had great potential for smuggling other things apart from guns, and so you used your Mafia connections . . .'

'Excuse me,' he said, putting down his glass. 'But this really has gone on too long already.' I thought he was going to bluster his innocence and throw me out. He wasn't. 'Your version of events is too simplistic. It ignores so many factors. It wasn't the idea of smuggling that suggested I should get involved. In many ways my sympathies have always been with the terrorists. I spent an undergraduate year in America, time off from Oxford; I was at Columbia University in '68. Do you know Columbia? It's in Harlem, a little oasis of civilized values in the midst of the dereliction and the ghettoes, or so we were told. But that was nonsense, as was clear to anyone with eyes to see. Columbia was the ghetto, a ghetto of privileged white parasites feeding off the sweat, blood and tears of the workers. Yes, '68 was a revelation to me. I sometimes think that had I been born thirty years earlier I might have become a Soviet agent like Philby and Blunt. That would have suited my temperament: I was too rich, and too English, to take part in riots. But I knew where my loyalties lay.

'And another thing. The smuggling was not done simply to make money, but rather to launder money. My involvement with the Accord was not a takeover; I offered my expertise. Many of the terrorist organizations within the Accord are capable of raising money through their various extra-legal activities, but the money so frequently needs to be rechannelled. Arms dealers are inclined to question the provenance of the cash with which they're paid; drug dealers in third world countries are not. The dirty money from the terrorists was used to buy drugs; money raised through the sale of drugs came in small, anonymous contributions which added together to make a fortune; we spent that fortune in the semi-legitimate world arms market. It worked splendidly, but as you can see, the drug-pushing was neither exploitation nor opportunism: it was an integral part of the whole operation.

'And thirdly I have no "Mafia" connections. I know businessmen from a wide variety of backgrounds, that is all.'

'If that's all, I'll carry on,' I said. The man and his motives may have been interesting but I wasn't in the mood to believe a word he said. I had things of my own to say. 'I also know how *Advanced Mathematical Tables* works, but that's too complicated to go into now. And finally I know you have decided to get out of the Cairo Accord for some reason, and to cover your retreat you are setting me up as a scapegoat, although, let's be honest, why anyone would believe I could organize the hundred-yard sprint in a dysentery ward I don't know.'

'You have a colourful, if convoluted, turn of phrase,' he said judiciously. 'And once more I am forced to correct you. Firstly, your suitability as a candidate for the post of Bigman is irrelevant.

We are not looking for a perfect match, we are looking for a fall-guy. You have been to some of the right places, met some of the right people, and won't be missed. The police need a name to put on their files and a body to put in their prisons – or graveyards – and you, as it happens, will do.

'The second point is my retirement. Perhaps I have already surprised you, Mr Diamond, with my reminiscences of student revolt in the sixties; if you have followed that, you will realize I would leave the business only for ethical reasons. The most profitable drugs in the world at the moment are on the Mosquito Coast to Florida trip, the Caribbean run. Naturally certain of those businessmen you refer to, with typical outsiders' inaccuracy, as "Mafia" have interests in that run. Naturally they have seen my method and they know it works. And naturally I will not be involved in an attempt to prop up the right-wing regimes of the Central Americas, nor to topple the Sandinistas in Nicaragua.'

I expect I looked sceptical. He drank a little more whisky and continued. 'You're right, of course. I did have other objections. Taxation in Britain is no longer punitive, and these offshore ventures are no longer so attractive. And the trouble with the drugs-and-arms business is that it is sordid. Too many adventurers like yourself get involved in it, and I find myself forced to rely on idiots like dear old Bendy or crooks like Flaherty. By the way, I suppose I should thank you for shooting Flaherty. He was becoming a major thorn in my side with his intrigues and double-dealings. Not a man to trust, I found.'

'It wasn't me who shot him,' I said, and then it was my turn to be gracious. 'I ought to thank you, in turn, for paying for my defence.'

This time, for the first time, he looked shocked by what I said. It was the first time he'd even looked interested, come to that. I was a sounding-board, there to receive rather than impart information. 'I had nothing to do with your defence!' he said. 'Good grief! I didn't even want you out of police custody; and had I done so I would have made sure the aid could never have been traced to me.'

'You'd better check some of the charitable trusts you support,' I told him.

He frowned, and then his face cleared. 'Ah! So the funds came from the Percy Bysshe Shelley Trust! I had already decided to stop my contribution – radicalism's a spent force, don't you know, an anachronism in these Thatcher-ridden days. That the Trust has actually helped you get your freedom doubles my resolution.'

I brushed this digression aside and returned to the main theme of our cosy chat. 'Are you telling me,' I was telling him, 'that you've acted with honourable motives throughout your involvement with the Cairo Accord?'

'Yes.'

I shook my head.

'You do not understand me, do you?' he said, accurately, and continued before I could reply. 'But then I don't understand you either. You come here. You tell me a story we both know to be true, and both know to be incredible. You lay all your cards on the table and leave nothing up your sleeve, yet seem to assume you will get out of here alive. You are a strange man, Mr Diamond.'

I shrugged. 'What have I got to lose?'

'You have your life to lose, Mr Diamond.'

'I lost that a long time ago.'

'Ah yes,' he said. 'I gather you were officially killed off in the desert.'

I shook my head. 'No. Before that. In a fishpond south-east of Derry.'

His hand patted his hair. 'Surely if that's your attitude you'd be an ideal fall-guy. Perhaps I can encourage you to play the part: you'll get plenty of respect in prison; I'm sure special facilities could be laid on, and I know we can smuggle in women and spirits, or harder drugs if they're to your taste. It really would be a weight off my shoulders if Bigman were captured.'

I shook my head. 'No thanks.'

'A pity. So what can I do for you? Why exactly are you here?'

'Curiosity, I expect. You've changed my life for me: you've even changed my bloody identity. You can't blame me for wanting to meet you!'

'Far from it. But is that all you want? What about justice, or money? Most people want the latter; you're an honourable man by your own lights though, and I thought you might be interested in justice.'

'Sure.' I tossed back the whisky, stood, and walked to the windows. Evening was being poured over Rome like liqueur on a fancy dessert, and the setting sun flambéed the skyline. Or so it seemed. 'I'm fascinated by justice.' I thought about the lady whose brains were blown out by the terrorist on the hijacked plane. I thought about Rebecca doing the same thing to Flaherty and wondered if that cause was just. I no longer knew. I still don't know. We were beyond the comfortable asylum of everyday life, where human behaviour is regulated by custom and convention; we were in the subterranean carpark beneath, where the light is the fleeting light of headlamps cutting the darkness and behind every concrete pillar is a guy with a knife.

'A penny for your thoughts,' suggested Pellon.

I looked up. It was hot in the sun. I began to sweat slightly. 'You'd never make a worse deal,' I told him. 'My thoughts are a nonsense.' Maybe it was the heat that made me fume. 'But then it's all a nonsense, isn't it? I've been looking for the sense in this business, expecting that somewhere there'll be a key, a secret, an answer. I thought you'd supply it. And instead you spout a load of crap about the spirit of '68 that explains nothing! Come on. Let's try again. Tell me: what's it all about?'

'Do you really want to know?' He joined me at the window. 'Look out there. Rome. The centre of the greatest empire and the greatest organized church the world has seen. What a wonderful sham! You've read Gibbon's *Decline and Fall*? How appropriate that the decline and fall of the Roman Empire should be catalogued by a man with a name like Gibbon. Did you know that the apes we know as "gibbons" were named after a man called Gibbon? And that the word "gibberish" derives from the chatter of those apes?'

I couldn't say I did. He continued with his trivia quiz. 'Have you read *The Waste Land*?' he asked. '"I think we are in rats' alley/

Where the dead men lost their bones." I don't believe in anything very much,' he went on, 'but I believe in that. We're in rats' alley.'

I had nothing much to say. What is the correct response when a psychopathic aristocrat quotes T. S. Eliot? He changed track. 'Do you know where Pellon is?' he asked.

I'd been able to answer the Art and Literature questions but Geography had me foxed. I shook my head.

'It's in Halifax,' he said. 'And do you know what George Savile, Marquis of Halifax in the eighteenth century, said?'

Now the questions were getting really tricky. I shook my head again, and watched the Roman sun set like a jelly.

'"There is no fundamental, but that every supreme power must be arbitrary."' He shook his head and smiled. 'I live by that maxim. I am a supreme power. I am an arbitrary one. I am arbitrary to maintain my supremacy, for consistency leads to predictability and predictability to weakness, but I am also arbitrary to suit my whims. Which is lucky for you, Mr Diamond. I have changed my mind about you. Major Fahd still has your passport, I believe. It will be returned to you. I have decided you would make a lousy fall-guy. I have decided to send you home.'

But I did not know where home was any more. I thought about London: smoke-filled snooker halls and queues in the rain; pavements slippery with cardboard cartons from fast-food shops; all-night Indian grocers with their shops wired in like a con- fessional; middle-aged Irishmen and middle-aged West Indians sitting either side of dingy saloon bars, wearing narrow-brimmed hats and reading the racing papers; lunchtime strippers with their breasts bobbing, unenthusiastically, a half-beat behind the music. I looked at Pellon. I thought about Derry: kids kicking footballs round uneven fields where the goals were burnt-out cars; a cold wind tugging the shawls of the sad old women; oranges banned from good Catholic homes; the coffins we shouldered like guns. He looked back at me. He was serious. I was going somewhere, but wherever it was it was no longer home.

Oh – shit.

TWENTY

'That's it, is it?' I asked. A tale told by an idiot, full of sex and violence, signifying nothing; a cock and bull story with less cock than bull.

'What more can you want?' he asked. 'You got involved in my affairs by chance. You wanted out. I'm letting you out and sending you home. I'll even provide a certain amount of money to cover your expenses.'

'Why?'

'An arbitrary whim. I like you, Mr Diamond, with your blundering through and your notion that there should be a meaning to things. Don't you know that life has no meaning; it is like me, arbitrary, powerful, contradictory, an accident of cosmology and bio-chemistry. It is also a mental construct. What we experience as "life" is something we invent in our heads from the information our faulty senses provide; it has very little to do with what is actually occurring, but it's all we've got and we're stuck with it. Likewise this question of "meaning". The only meaning life can have is the meaning we chose to impose upon it, and because no single meaning, except maybe religious faith, is sufficient to cover the facts, the only meaning is in the search for meaning. But I see you are losing interest.'

'Am I? How rude.' But survival is more potent than ontology any day. 'How do you know I won't go straight to the police when I leave here? Or when I get back to England?' I asked.

'Mr Diamond. I have been consistently under-estimating you since you first became involved in my organization. I think now it is time to give a certain credit to your intelligence. There are a number of reasons you will not go to the police. They would not believe you, and any statement you made would only implicate you further, whilst by keeping quiet you will find my influence sufficient to extricate you. Equally, no purpose would be served even if you succeeded in turning me in, as I have relinquished the role of Bigman. And finally, were you to attempt to inform the police of my activities you'd be dead within days. Does that answer your question?'

'It begs another. How do I know you won't have me killed anyway?'

'You don't.'

Well, I couldn't quibble with that. The interview was over and the guards were summoned. 'Your gun, I believe,' said Pellon, but it wasn't, it was Fahd's.

'Keep it,' I said.

The lift arrived and its suede-coated doors opened smoothly. Two security guards bulked out and parted like curtains; behind them, on the far wall of the lift, was a still life, seventeenth-century Dutch at a guess, depicting cream carnations in a pewter vase. 'Mr Diamond is going down with you,' said Pellon to the guards, and they turned politely and let me lead them back the way they'd come.

They followed me in. No button was pressed but the lift began to move. There was nothing else to look at so I looked at the Dutch painting, but at close range the petals and stalks dissolved into meaningless grey, cream and white brushstrokes.

I walked through the foyer, through the elegant doors and down the steps. A scooter roared along the road. The beam of its light transfixed the night for a moment like a moth on a board. I stood still, expectantly, but nobody shot me or tossed a grenade. Instead transistorized music popped from the scooter, and I heard an innocent guilty giggle from the girl riding pillion as they passed. I sighed for the lovers, and the lovers I had lost.

I got back to Fahd's car and drove off. It was too late to make my meal with Angelo on the Estrolti, and I called him at home to apologize. He asked where I had been and I told him a lie. 'I'm glad you telephoned,' he said. 'I was going to ask you where you were staying.'

It was a good point. 'I haven't decided,' I said, which was true.

'You must stay with me.' Either the man was well named – I'd just stood him up for dinner and here he was willing to put me up for the night – or there was something suspicious going on. But I went along with him despite my suspicions – I had bugger-all else to do – and followed the directions he had given me over the phone.

Angelo had a nice apartment in a mixed neighbourhood, where strings of washing hung over the street and the only objects of architectural interest were the fire escapes. I parked the Merc on a piece of waste land and locked it carefully. I wasn't going to use it again, but I didn't want joyriders to nick it: Fahd would probably like it back.

'My girlfriend, Isa,' said Angelo, introducing a pretty young lady in intelligent specs. 'She is a scientist.'

'I'm pleased to meet you,' she said.

'And now, have you eaten?' he asked.

'I'm all right,' I told him.

'I did not ask this. I asked "Have you eaten?"'

'Well, no then.'

He and Isa smiled cheerfully. 'Then we shall make a meal for you,' she said.

They busied themselves in the kitchen. There was a CD on the player, some opera or another, and when it got to the famous bit – in English it's about tiny hands being frozen – they joined in, in Italian of course, singing from the kitchen over the sizzle of frying and boiling. The meal was pasta, and superb.

I want to be Angelo when I grow up.

The next day Angelo went to work on my case, Isa went off to her lab, and I hung around the apartment, feeling at peace with the world and listening to a lot of Puccini, partly because I was getting to like it and mostly because I didn't dare try to change the

CD. In the afternoon, because it was hot, I went for a stroll, had a thick black coffee, which tasted of earwax, on the pavement of a nearby café, and rehearsed for my London life.

Isa came home before Angelo and put the Pet Shop Boys on the CD player. 'Not Puccini?' I asked.

'The Pet Shop Boys have a tighter dynamic range and a greater rhythmic congruence, which wakes me up after work.' I expect this way of talking is known as the scientist's retort. 'Besides, I prefer them.'

Angelo telephoned. He was going to be delayed. We should eat without him. And so we did. He arrived at about eight, ecstatic and flustered. 'What is it?' asked Isa.

'The case! The case against Jack! They have dropped it!'

'Amazing!' she said. 'I'm so glad! On what grounds?'

'Lack of evidence!'

'Wonderful!'

'Wonderful!'

'Fabulous!'

'Fabulous!'

'Amazing!'

'Amazing!'

We'd had that one before but I decided I wouldn't remind them. They were so happy for me. I wasn't. But I didn't want to spoil their celebration, which they thought was mine, and I joined in the fun.

There was a parcel for me the next morning, with my passport, some cash, an inventory, and a handwritten note bearing a formal signature: Mohammed el Fahd ould Ely ould Ahkmed, Major of the Patriotic Qafadyan Armed Forces. The note was weird. Fahd hoped his car had been of use to me, and apologized for the petrol tank being half-empty! After a moment's thought I realized what I was reading. It was a naked statement of Pellon's clout. If Fahd could write this crap after I'd nicked his prize Merc, it said between the lines, then think what could happen to me.

I opened the passport. Jack Diamond looked out at me, hairy

but unbearded, with fat black Irish sideburns. I hadn't seen him for a long time. I still didn't know if I liked him.

This was only one of the worries that occupied my flight home. There were others. I'd almost got used to planes by now, which isn't the same as saying I liked them. But when I totalled up my worries I seemed to have even more than on my flight to Thessalonika all those months ago. My most significant, pointless worry was the old *Waiting for the Toilet* line, 'What is to be done?' (In that remarkably inept drama, incidentally, the answer was the same one I came up with, i.e. nothing.)

The plane landed at Heathrow. I'd last seen my car at Gatwick. By now, though I didn't yet know it, the Astra was a burnt-out wreck on a derelict site in Liverpool. There was no one waiting to meet me, no one I could even tell I was home. I took the tube back to Edgware Road, and got the keys to my bedsit back from Ulrich, my Ugandan landlord. Ulrich was annoyed with me for being away so long – 'Hey, where'd you been man?' – so I shovelled a handful of Lord Pellon's cash into his hands in a successful attempt to relieve the situation. The bedsit was much as I'd left it, except for the pile of credit card bills behind the door. Last time I'd been there Mulligan's brains were smeared across the room and Flaherty had been nursing an injured hand. Now the place was clean, though musty. I opened a window and let in the smells of London. There were tins still in the cupboard under the sink. I dusted them off but could not face opening one yet.

Outside it was lunchtime and the pubs were open. A little heap of cash had survived Ulrich's onslaught, not enough to make me rich but enough to pay off the credit cards and still buy me lunch, so I wandered down to the Tar and Feather.

It had been tarted up again in my absence. This happens from time to time: about five years ago the brewery spent a fortune transforming it from a typical London pub into 'A Typical London Pub', which meant tossing out all the formica and linoleum and bringing in lots of bits of demolished churches: stained glass, pew rails and brass. Since then, the brewery periodically appoints a new manager with the task of shoving the Tar and Feather upmarket, though God knows the only effective way to smarten up the clientele would be a sheepdip. When I walked in that day for my first bite of English food since slightly longer than I don't know when, they offered me an 'Executive Ploughman's Lunch'.

I passed time and water indiscriminately. First the minutes, then the hours, days and weeks. The trees started losing their leaves, becoming filament and filigree. A journalist called round. He wanted the story of how I had escaped from the hijack. 'We wanted your personal story,' he said. 'Have you any comment on the official version?' But I didn't even know there had been an official version so I just opted for a typically Irish evasion. 'No,' I said, which was true. He went away unsatisfied but that was tough.

And that's how things were for a long time. The evenings grew colder. I found myself returning to my old haunts: Ginger's Snooker Emporium, Maurie's, the pubs, the DHSS and the cafés. Little happened to disturb my state, which was boredom or tranquillity depending on how many I'd had. One day, the same day the insurance money on my Astra came through, I saw a magazine on the top shelf of a nearby newsagent's. Rebecca was on the cover. I looked inside, recognizing the curves and hollows of her flesh, but the text didn't tell me if she was married yet. I expect she was. Constein seemed the determined type. I bought a copy. The newsagent shook his head in disapproval and tutted as I handed over my £1.50, but I didn't care if he thought *Penthouse* was better value. And just a few days ago, in the *Guardian*, I saw an item on the international news page: a wanted terrorist and drug-runner, known as 'Bigman', had been arrested in Leipzig. There was a smudged photograph showing the suspect going into court. It certainly wasn't Pellon; it looked more like Chambers. I wondered.

And what happened the day after that, the day before yesterday? All I can remember is going to church and lighting a candle for my dad; there must have been more, and it must have been riveting.

Of the day that followed that, yesterday, my memory is sharper.

I'd already decided to get a replacement car with the insurance so I went down to Connor's Showroom. The 'Showroom' title is a bit ambitious for a prefabricated hut in the middle of a lump of waste ground, but he has a reputation for cheapness and for supporting the cause. A wispy-looking lad in a sheepskin was leaning against an old Rover, picking his teeth with his thumbnail. The sheepskin suggested that he worked there – Connor liked his boys to look respectable – so I went over. We recognized one another simultaneously. He was the wispy youth who'd so nearly beaten me at snooker all that time ago; he told me who I was with a surprised cry, but I already knew and was unimpressed. I was just glad I'd met him there and not at a snooker hall. But any pleasure soon left me. The kid looked at me like I'd got the plague, dashed into the prefab, and fetched out Connor and two of the boys.

While I, all innocence, just stood there.

I'd never actually met Connor before but I knew him straight away, with his sheepskin coat, flat cap and his fat turd-shaped cigar. 'Diamond,' he said, all the Irish knocked from his voice by the years. 'I want a word with you.'

I shrugged. 'Okay. What about?'

'Grab him!'

A couple of Connor's boys pinned my arms and held me. Across the yard I could see children playing. They watched the heavies lay into me and didn't do a thing to help.

'What's going on?' I asked.

'Let's cut his prick off,' suggested one of the muscles.

'Yeah,' agreed the other with relish. They started tugging at my belt.

'Stop!' It was Connor's voice, authoritative and loud; the lads obeyed, reluctantly. 'I don't want to have to look at his lousy prick. Just get rid of him.'

'What's it all about? There must be an explanation,' I said. I'd been in worse messes. I wasn't panicking yet.

Connor came up to me, stuck a finger up my nose, and twisted.

I followed as far as I could without my head snapping off. 'Listen, big guy.' It seems he meant me. 'You know my daughter, right.'

'I've never met her,' I said. The finger up my nose was twisted further. The damage Flaherty had done had at least been instant.

'Liar. You're the father of her child and you know it.'

'I've never sodding met her!'

'Hear that lads?' asked Connor rhetorically. 'She's eight months up the stick and he's never met her. Perhaps he thinks it's the fucking Immaculate Conception?'

'I still say cut his prick off,' volunteered the muscle.

'Who's up the stick?' I asked, a little desperately and very nasally.

'My fucking daughter,' said Connor. 'Kelly. The one you've never fucking met.'

'Kelly?' It rang a bell.

Connor nodded sagely and removed his finger. Blood came out with it, tasting metallic as it ran down my lip. 'Kelly Connor. Sweetest loveliest girl born this side of Kensington till you got your filthy hands on her.'

'Kelly,' I repeated. The girl at Maurie's. I got the feeling that telling her father she was more available than Mars Bars wouldn't improve my prospects any.

'Worked it out now, have you? Remembered her?' Connor was all charm. 'Maybe you'll remember this!' His knee came up and hit me full in the balls. I saw the world through rose-coloured agony and choked back the vomit. Tears ran down my face and mixed with the blood.

'Chop off his prick,' said the heavy again. He wasn't a great one for originality.

Connor ignored him. 'Catholic girl she is, and my only daughter. And you fucking fuck her! Bastard!'

'Do you want me to marry her? Is that it?' I was still married. I didn't care. I'd have married Connor himself if he'd wanted.

This time it was his fist, in my stomach, and this time I was unable to hold back the vomit. 'Mucky bugger,' commented one of the muscles, wiping his shoe on the back of my leg.

'Hold him there,' said Connor. 'I'll get the Jag.'

He reversed up and opened the car boot. There was a length of rope for just such an emergency, and they wrapped it round and round me. 'Gag,' Connor said.

He fetched some Sellotape from the prefab while the heavies took off my socks. The socks were bundled together in a pair, one poking out of the other like a circumcision, and then shoved into my mouth. They tasted foul; they tasted of me. Then the tape was looped over my head and I was bundled into the boot.

It was a long drive. I thought of Kelly; I thought of my deserted Derry daughter of that age. I thought a bit about the child in Kelly's womb too, but not for long. It couldn't have been mine because I'd been given the snip. I hoped it would be black.

We arrived somewhere remote and windswept. It was getting dark. On a road beneath us I saw headlamps three lanes wide, and a tall blue sign saying M25. One heavy took my feet, the other my shoulders. 'Lay him by the side of the hole,' ordered Connor.

I was put on the ground. It would have been good to explain to Connor, tell him about my vasectomy, save my life, but my socks, wrinkled like my scrotum, filled my mouth. I could see the hole, gaping black in the night, beside my head. Connor stood above me. 'They'll start work at seven this morning,' he said. 'You'll not have so long to wait.'

He rested a foot on my shoulder and shoved. I skidded, rolled a few inches, and tumbled painfully into this hole. It's daylight now. They've started to pour the cement. To begin with it has no force; it slaps the sides of the hole and slides, slippily, grittily, down the rough shaft. But then it gets stronger. It lurches, spurts, and settles finally for a steady grey spume that arches above the shoring and seems, to my damaged mind, to be something to do with whales. I had never thought concrete could have such significance.

Then there is an inch of it, and rising, at the foot of the shaft. It traps and stills the leaves. I bend my neck to keep my head out of the muck but as the inch becomes two, and then three, I can't keep my face up any longer. The concrete reaches my left eye, and

I have to close it. A first taste gets to my mouth, granular between my teeth. I had expected the concrete to crush me, but as more gets in between my teeth and the sock or plugs clammily on my nose, I realize I'm going to drown. The thought makes the concrete weigh heavy on my head and my dreams. I feel myself going under.

I kick off my shoes and dive again. My mouth and eyes are clogged, but this time I find him, hold him. We burst through for air. The shore is far away. 'Michael,' I manage to say; 'Already,' he replies. Then we are dragged beneath the grey once again. We are going under for that third time when men drown. 'Michael,' I tell him with my mind, for my mouth will not work beneath the grey. 'Dada,' he says and then 'Dada'.

I'm just a man with private parts to play with and public parts to play. I can do nothing to save him. But I shall never leave him again. And so we cling together until, secure in each other and safe from the world, we drown.

ABOUT THE AUTHOR

Richard Burns was born in Sheffield in 1958 and educated at the universities of Lancaster and Sheffield. Among his earlier novels are *A Dance For The Moon* and *The Panda Hunt*. He lives in Sussex.